The Rovan Trap
(Book 13 of the PIT series)
by Michael McCloskey
Copyright 2019 Michael McCloskey

Learn more about Michael McCloskey's works at
www.squidlord.com

Cover art by Stephan Martiniere

Chapter 1

Marcant put his hand on the back of his neck to work the kinks out. Though he had complained irritably just minutes before when he rose from his control throne, he supposed that incarnate meetings did have certain benefits. Without the meeting, he would have no compelling reason to leave his chair on an off-workout day. The official reasoning was that Terran psychology reacted better to incarnate meetings, at least when the participants spent a large portion of their time working with virtual interfaces.

At least I'll be listening to Barrai rather than getting beaten by her, he thought.

He walked down a corridor of the *Sharplight*, headed for the mess where the meeting was scheduled. The half of the PIT team aboard, consisting of himself, Barrai, Telisa, and Maxsym, had taken to doing meetings in the mess to knock out two incarnate tasks at once: eat and meet. Barrai called it an 'E&M' and Marcant supposed the term came from the Space Force.

Marcant arrived. He spotted Barrai already eating at a long, low table. The others had not made it yet, so Marcant got a bowl of intertwined protein and resistant-starch noodles. He got comfortable and ingested half his food by the time Telisa sat down with her usual multi-plate meal. Maxsym was ready a minute later.

Telisa got right to the point. She looked at Barrai.

"We've been looking forward to your report," Telisa said.

"Thank you, TM. As you all know, it's been an immense amount of work to recover from the damage sustained by the rovling incursion."

Barrai sent everyone a pointer. Marcant effortlessly opened it in his PV and gave it a large share of his attention. Various synthetic views of the *Sharplight* flitted by as Barrai talked.

"The *Sharplight* was designed to repair itself. We have sophisticated manufacturing capabilities on board. For the most part, this is a success story. Nevertheless, there are some components we can't build at the original fidelity, and some others that we could build but don't have enough raw materials for."

"All essential systems are at one hundred percent. The ship's many redundancies are back in order and ready to gracefully handle new battle damage, if it comes to that. One of our high power weapons took a direct hit to the emitter, so I had to replace the Vovokan components with Terran ones, giving us a twelve percent degradation, but amortized across our total firepower, this is less than one percent of our capability for long range energy strikes."

Marcant had forgotten that the *Sharplight* had any Vovokan components at all. It was a part of Shiny's upgrades to the Space Force to prepare for war with the Quarus.

The PV display changed radically, shifting to a robot factory and a side selector offering many machine design templates.

"We've replaced our robot army with a new one at twice the numbers: we have over 600 soldier machines on board."

Telisa clapped. "I'm celebrating in Magnus's place," she explained.

"The metal supplies we stole from the Rovan outpost were very helpful in constructing our new army; however, it's important to note that the materials are substandard. We've created several types of steel from the bars we lifted, but let's face it: iron alloys and composites are too heavy for optimal combat performance. Of course, I've mitigated this by strategically adding components made from lighter and stronger modern materials."

Telisa looked concerned.

"What is the combat effectiveness of our new army compared to the old one, given that the individual machines are inferior but we have greater numbers?"

"Approximately half again as strong as what we had in the last attack," Barrai said. When Telisa seemed to accept this, she continued.

"That covers our repairs and replenishment. Now I'll move on to the work I've done to improve our chances in any future battle with the Rovans."

The PV changed again. The *Sharplight* disappeared, to be replaced by schematics of Rovan torpedoes.

Marcant perked up. He had not expected this.

"I've completed an analysis of the Rovan incursion capsules and determined how much energy it takes to disable them. Turns out we wasted twenty percent of our point defense power last time. Most of our shots were overkills. I've reduced the Rovan point defense settings for *Sharplight* down fifteen percent, to account for capsule variations or possible upgrades on their part. If we're attacked again, the point defenses will do the same job with less power draw."

"Excellent work," Telisa said.

Barrai continued after only a brief pause.

"Thank you, TM. My next improvement springs from an analysis of Rovan breach sites on the hull."

3

The feed changed to a three-dimensional model of the *Sharplight* with hull breaches marked with red dots.

"These are the sites that were struck by capsules in the last incursion. Notice the symmetrical pattern to the chosen breach points. These were *not* randomly selected. It looks like the Rovans wanted to inject rovlings as far into the ship as possible. They avoided extremities and favored sunken areas and niches."

The presentation ran images of a series of new hardpoints within the *Sharplight*.

"I've used this to predict future breach points and harden them, both in terms of armoring the hull and by adding laser emplacements to key interior sites around these preferred breach points."

Nice. I feel safer already.

Since Adair was not present, there was no witty reply. Marcant missed his AI friends, even though one of them had turned out to be less than loyal.

"That concludes the current measures I have in place. I'd now like to propose another project to enhance our security."

Marcant was already impressed. Now his curiosity was piqued.

I actually thought this would be dull.

A new pane opened to reveal Barrai's project. He saw a sophisticated set of designs for a familiar looking combat robot: a battle sphere.

"When we integrated Achaius and Adair into the Vovokan battle spheres, we learned a lot about their design. Though our current best methods for emulating Vovokan technology fall short here and there, we can construct three of these combat machines with seventy percent the battle effectiveness of the Vovokan originals."

"There is a cost to pay for this project, but I hope to convince you it is small. The *Sharplight* was designed to house a battalion of biological and robotic troops; some of that capability was destroyed. We can cannibalize the extra life support and power systems dedicated to housing large numbers of troops in the ship to build these combat machines. *Sharplight* would still be capable of comfortably transporting fifty Terrans on long voyages."

"That does seem worth it," Telisa said. "I have a question. When we return to Blackhab, will we still be able to restore that capability?"

"Yes TM. A single trip to Blackhab would be sufficient to restore what we lost."

"Then go ahead with it," Telisa said.

Barrai nodded. "Any questions?"

"Are there any other areas where we remain worse off?" Marcant asked.

Barrai nodded.

"We've lost many convenient services as I mentioned before," she said. "We can no longer support four hundred people on the ship. We don't have many grenades left. It would be a major project to get to where we could replace those we've lost with new ones comparable to the originals manufactured by the Space Force."

"We can build Vovokan battle spheres but not grenades?" Marcant asked.

"Both are major projects," Barrai said. "It's harder to build a top-notch smart grenade than you think, especially with limited supplies of explosive, acceleration-resistant brains, hardened security on the control systems, and particularly the blast-cone control technology. Those grenades are able to explode at any given millisecond with a dynamically chosen distribution of energy channeled in any combination of directions without having to adjust facing before detonation. Still, in the end, it's mostly about the materials at hand. I have what I need to repurpose serious power systems and build the energy emitters that a Vovokan battle sphere needs. I don't happen to have a lot of what I need to make the grenades."

"Battle spheres it is, then," Telisa said. "Three of them."

"Aye, TM."

Marcant realized he had stopped eating while watching the information panes march by in his link. He resumed in a thoughtful mood. Back on Earth, he had known some sharp people, but Telisa had managed to put together a team of incredibly intelligent, driven individuals.

The question was, the next time six thousand rovlings decided to invite themselves aboard the *Sharplight*, would they be as impressed with Barrai's preparations as he was?

Chapter 2

Magnus contemplated the interior of his spacious cell. The smooth, gray walls rose on all four sides to about three times his own height, then terminated at a featureless white ceiling. A transparent cylinder of water half a meter long had been provided for him. It sat in one corner. One wall gave off a dull light starting at its first meter of height and stopping somewhere about two meters higher, like a heavily frosted window. Magnus suspected that wall might be transparent in the other direction, as sometimes he thought he sensed shadows moving beyond it.

As he looked at the suspected window, a new thought came to him:

It's like that cell we saw in the shipyard... except I'm on the inside.

Magnus stood. He examined the walls in light of his new realization.

Am I inside a force field?

Magnus still had his combat knife strapped to his leg. The rovlings had not taken it from him, in fact, they had taken nothing from him when they captured him and carried him to the Rovan battleship. His force field and stealth sphere were critically low on power, and his ammunition had run out.

He slipped the knife out and struck the pommel against the wall.

It produced a dull thud rather than a sharp clang.

Magnus frowned. He reversed the blade and tried the point. It slid one way, then another when he tried to drive it straight into the wall.

Seems like it. Great. It'll be even harder to escape than I thought.

Magnus walked over and picked up the cylinder for a drink. Part of its lid lifted up to reveal a stiff flap, which Magnus had learned could be pried open to let the contents dribble out.

They know I need water. They mean for me to live.

Magnus felt an urge to yell. He had already gone over the cell centimeter by centimeter several times. He had done exercises, gone over some of the data in his link cache, and accessed his equipment manuals from the computers embedded in every single item.

Magnus sat down and took the tiny alien artifact from his pack.

It glowed weakly. The surface felt smooth and cool.

What are you?

"What are you?" he repeated aloud. "Can you hear me?"

It's probably a grenade. I'll blow myself up in here.

Magnus stood and paced. He stopped suddenly as the artifact glowed brighter in his hand. Magnus waited, staring at it. There was no further change in its luminosity.

"You hear me?"

Nothing happened.

"Go dim if you hear me," he said.

The glow did not change.

He took another step. The light wavered. He moved it left and right. More variance. He brought it over to the wall. The brightness intensified.

It glows brighter near the force field!

Magnus heard a clanking noise. He spun around, searching for the source.

A low opening had appeared in a corner of his cell opposite the lit wall. A rovling advanced, pushing a flat plate of metal before it. A round bowl lay in the center. Then the machine darted back out and the doorway flickered.

Force field.

Then the lit area behind the flickering lowered, and the corner looked like his plain cell wall again.

Well, it's not hard to interpret all this. Feeding the prisoner.

Magnus knelt down and examined the bowl. It had chunks of gray matter in it. Magnus smelled it. The odor was not good or bad, just unrecognizable.

Magnus took out a food bar from his pack and ripped one large bite out of it, then placed the remainder on the flat metal surface. He hoped a sample of Terran food would be helpful for his captors. Magnus wondered what lengths they might go to get it right; were they interested in perfecting his food? Or would they simply feed him gruel until he became hungry enough to eat it?

When he stood again, he saw a change had occurred in the other back corner from the lit wall. The floor had turned black in an area the same size as his metal plate: maybe two-thirds of a meter square.

What now?

He warily walked over to the corner. A flicker made him decide the area was still covered with a force field. Below that, he saw only darkness.

Toilet? Or is it just a rovling tube?

Magnus supposed it would not be long before he would be forced to assume the former.

Rovans are living beings… do they have to excrete anything besides gas? Lee said the Celarans just shed wastes in their skin, because the only thing they eat is the sap and it's an almost pure carbohydrate.

Magnus set the artifact down near the force field, hoping that the glow might mean it was gathering energy. If it was something useful, he'd rather have it charged. He wondered again if it was a small bomb.

"Magnus?"

It was Yat. The link connection was tenuous. It reported that the underlying transport would send messages several times until the other side received the data in its entirety.

"What? Yat? Where are you?"

There was no answer. Magnus scrambled to stand.

"Yat, can you hear me?"

"Magnus? You're alive!"

"Yes. Yes."

"Good. We're here."

"In a cell?" Magnus asked.

"Yes."

"How much of this food have you eaten?" Magnus asked.

"Food? We only have water."

"What? They aren't giving you these gray cubes?" Magnus asked.

There was no answer.

"Yat? Yat? Are they giving you anything?"

The link connection was gone. Magnus paced back and forth, waiting for it to re-establish itself, but it did not come back. He tried putting his head against the force field. He walked over to the artifact and snatched it up, then walked back and forth again. Still nothing.

No food? Are they treating the prisoners differently? Perhaps to learn something.

Magnus sighed. He knew Telisa would come for them, but he could only hope she did not end up in another cell like his.

Michael McCloskey

Chapter 3

Imanol opened his eyes. The first thing he saw was a sinuous green dragon.

"Hello!" the dragon said.

Imanol ignored the creature. It was just too nonsensical to process. Instead, he looked around.

A tall gray column rose to a high ceiling on his left. Before him and extending to his right, rows of chairs faced the platform where he stood. Through three open doorways, he spotted green vines and open sky.

He looked down at himself. He wore a glossy new Veer suit in black and silver. He reached for his pistols, but found none on his belt.

Imanol's eyes returned to the dragon.

"What happened?" he asked aloud.

"They say you should sit for some kinds of news…"

"Is that why there are so many damn chairs in this room? Is this a bad news room?"

"No. It's just that I have to tell you something..."

"Hit me, Snake."

"You're back from the dead! You were a data pattern inside of the Trilisk column. It's restored you to… life."

"I'm just a simple frontier merc. Your Trilisk artifact frightens and confuses me. As do big green snakes."

Imanol's hand searched for a pistol again, almost on its own.

"I'm not a snake. Just a little dragon named Taishi. And I think you're Imanol!" The creature flashed rows of pointy teeth.

This snake is entirely too happy about things in general.

"I think I'm Imanol, too. *Why* am I back from the dead?"

"Telisa asked me to retrieve her team members."

"Oh yeah?" Imanol laughed. It sounded a little unstable to his ears. "Then where are the others? Who else bit it besides me?"

"I'm not sure how many more the column has... but I'm expecting Cilreth, Caden, and Siobhan. Telisa said Jason was a stretch goal."

"Stretch goal. Right."

Imanol leaned in a little and whispered. "Hey! Am I... you know?" He started flexing his arm and wriggling his fingers.

Taishi's exotic dragon brows furrowed.

"No, I don't know."

"Am I... *you know*... Trilisk Special Forces?"

"What an intriguing question!" Taishi said. "I wish I knew what it meant."

Imanol saw something flit by an open doorway in the distance. He knelt and moved away, toward the cover of a line of chairs.

"What's wrong?"

"I saw something fly by over there... something big!"

"Oh. Remain calm. That was a Celaran."

"Oh? We finally met some of those?"

"Yes. They're our allies. And very peaceful," Taishi said.

Suddenly an elegant woman with silver and black hair stood nearby. She wore a Veer suit like Imanol's.

"By the tentacle! Cilreth!" exclaimed Imanol.

Cilreth dropped to all fours and crawled over to Imanol where he knelt.

"Why are we covering?" she whispered nervously.

"I saw a flying alien. But Snake here says they're our friends. Do you know?"

"Celarans? Yes, they're friendly. But I don't know... the snake."

"I don't either," Imanol said. He straightened up, then slowly came to his feet, watching the door in the distance.

"Okay then... flying thing good," he said.

"You trust her," Taishi said. "So you recognize her, right? Can you remember everything?"

"That depends on what 'everything' is," he said. "But I recognize the Twitch Queen, here."

"Cilreth, is that you? Imanol!" a female voice said aloud.

Imanol and Cilreth turned to see Caden and Siobhan behind them.

"Wunderkind... Fast n' Frightening. Welcome to the chair room party," he said.

Caden raised his hand, palm up, stared at it, then clenched his fist. "Are we...?"

"Nope, I don't think so," Imanol said.

"You're all brand-new!" Taishi said enthusiastically.

Imanol raised his hand and hooked his thumb back toward the dragon.

"Please tell me this one didn't join the team?"

Michael McCloskey

Chapter 4

Hisss. Snap. Hisss.

Telisa shot six rovlings in three different directions in less than a second. She kept her laser pistol raised, ready for more. The scrabbling sounds of more approaching rovlings emanated from the pipes before her.

"We have a serious anomaly," Barrai said. "Our spinner has slowed for unknown reasons. We're no longer making significant headway toward our destination."

Telisa halted her pseudo-VR session and pulled up her visor, revealing the padded training room around her.

"It's not me," Telisa clarified. "Where are we?"

"On course, but this is deep space. Scans reveal many artificial objects out here."

Ships? In deep space?

Before Telisa could inquire about the absorption signatures, Barrai continued.

"We're receiving a Terran signal!" Barrai sent a pointer out to the team channel.

It was a message from Adair.

"This place is a trap. That big ship is a Rovan battleship. If you came in *Sharplight*, prepare for battle—I don't think *Sharplight* can hide from it."

Telisa dropped her pseudo-VR gear and ran out as the message continued.

"Magnus, Arakaki, and Yat were outside the ship investigating the wrecks when rovlings came and surrounded them. I was simultaneously engaged by Rovan ships. I think Magnus, at least, might still be alive. I caught a message from an attendant that showed him being captured in his force field. If you end up getting cornered, keep some power aside for the force field. I theorize that the rovlings will treat you like a captured Rovan if you have a screen on when the fight's over."

By the Five… the others never made it any farther than this! And we've been dallying back at the binary system!

"Send a message to Blackhab. Warn them there's a trap here," Telisa ordered. She hurried toward her quarters, planning to grab her weapons and equipment. She searched for the battleship Adair had mentioned.

The tactical showed one huge ship out there; Telisa assumed this was the Rovan dreadnought. Details were scarce this early on, but Barrai was already training sensors on the reported enemy.

"Adair managed to avoid being captured? Is the *Iridar* destroyed?" asked Maxsym on the team channel.

"The *Iridar* is out there," Barrai said. "The message included its location. It must be stealthed, as our routine scans did not reveal it."

The ship appeared on the tactical.

Adair could not save them? It sounded like the rovlings showed up unexpectedly…

Telisa did not blame Adair for being unable to protect the other team. She felt only anger at herself for splitting everyone up in the first place, then taking too long to attempt to reunite with them.

"We're sensing activity from that Rovan battleship," Barrai said. "It knows we're here."

A response is coming. I have to figure out how to get Magnus back from an alien battleship.

Telisa's first impulse was to order Barrai to drop her off and pull away from the area. She forced herself to think longer, even though a Rovan attack could be underway. She arrived at her quarters and started arming herself while thinking furiously.

"Is the spinner capable of getting *Sharplight* out of here?" Telisa demanded.

"No. It's disabled... Rovan ships are emerging from the battleship."

"Remember last time? We need to start shooting now," Marcant said. His statement did not really apply, since they were way out of range, but Telisa understood his sentiment. If they were going to succeed, an active defense would be necessary.

"I need to go and get the rest of our team out of there," Telisa said on the channel.

"Go. I'll lead them on a merry chase," Barrai vowed. "When they come in here, I have plenty of surprises for them."

"I want to help," Marcant said. "We go in together, again. We can save them."

How can I refuse his help? He's an asset when it comes to poking around Rovan places.

"Maxsym, choose a ship," Telisa said.

"I prefer the *Iridar*," Maxsym said.

It did not surprise her. The *Iridar* was both currently undetected and also where Maxsym had performed most of his research.

"Can't the *Sharplight* defend itself? You don't need to be here, Lieutenant," Telisa said.

"TM. Please. You heard Adair's message. As long as I keep some juice for my personal shield, they'll just capture me."

"That was only a theory. It didn't even see if Yat and Arakaki are dead or alive."

"And after capture, what then?" Marcant interjected. "When the power runs out and the field goes down, do they rip you to shreds?"

Telisa's faced pinched. The thought of Magnus...

Not again. I can't face this again.

"That's just the last fallback," Barrai said. "TM, I've worked hard to improve our defenses. Let me draw them away so that you can go in after Magnus!"

Telisa tried to be objective. Was Barrai offering to sacrifice herself? No. She believed her improvements would make her invincible. And even though Barrai refused to contemplate defeat, if the *Sharplight* was seized, there was a chance that Barrai would be captured alive.

"How can we do that? We lost all our shuttles in the last fight when we had to eject them to absorb some of the missiles," Maxsym said.

"We have space suits and our attendants can add range and speed," Marcant pointed out to Maxsym.

"Maxsym, Marcant, get your gear. We're leaving now. Maxsym, no time to pack any sampling tools or analysis equipment. Just grab your Veer, OCPs, weapons, and a bunch of ammo, then meet me here," she said, sending a pointer to a shuttle bay. "Barrai, stall them. Fight them. But if all is lost, use your stealth sphere to get out, or surrender with your Rovan force field on."

"Thank you, TM," Barrai said. "I'll keep our ship safe. Bring back the others."

I will. But I don't think there will be a Sharplight to bring them back to.

Chapter 5

Magnus fell in and out of sleep on the floor of his cell. He had counted off five days on his link so far. He wondered if he would be in the cell for years. That tortured thought poked and prodded at him to rise and do something. He pried himself to his feet and examined his surroundings yet again.

The corner with the black square of floor had indeed proven to be a place to deposit anything he wanted to be rid of. After some amount of time, inanimate things would fall through the force field into the hole below. His own limbs refused to go through it, even though he had tried standing on it perfectly still for a long time. Though it was less convenient than even a Vovokan sand toilet, he felt grateful that the cell had that functionality. A Celaran-designed prison cell might well have lacked any such feature entirely.

The artifact he had collected from the dead hulk still sat nearby, lit with an internal white light.

A long, ghostly shape appeared across the room out of thin air. Magnus caught his breath. A low, translucent wall now spanned the room, cutting it roughly in half. He watched it for a while, but it did not change. Magnus walked up to the knee-high wall and examined it. The wall was thick on one end, over a meter deep, but it thinned as it proceeded across the room until it was less than a centimeter thick at the other end.

He extended a glove from his Veer suit and tested it with the protected hand. It felt very smooth and very solid. *Force field?*

Magnus paced beside the wall for a time. What did it mean? It was too low to block his movement to the far side of the room. Why did its width vary? He had no answers.

Finally, Magnus sat on the middle of the wall.

If this thing disappears, I'm going to flop epically, he thought. He was not really concerned since his Veer suit would protect him from a wide range of mishaps.

He racked his brain to figure out why this wall had appeared.

It's probably a behavioral experiment. Something wants to know how I'll respond.

Magnus stood back up. He turned and tried to push the wall, but it would not budge.

So should I respond as a normal Terran would? Or mislead them? If they're dangerous to Terrans and Celarans, I should guide them astray. Make them think we're different than we are. But we have some evidence that the Rovans are not inherently xenophobic.

Finally he stepped away and sat across the room facing the ghostly wall with his back against the gray wall of his cell.

The wall before him shimmered for a moment. Magnus rose again and stepped over to inspect it. The wall had chosen a medium thickness this time, and the top edge facing him had rounded itself. To his right, the edge was rounder, but to his left it slowly disappeared until the edge was a perfect sharp corner.

Magnus felt the edge with his hand. It was very smooth.

Force field wall in my cell... but I can easily slip over it. A repetition of the difference left to right, though... that means something...

Magnus turned and sat again. He wondered if the Rovans were studying his movements and physiology. After a few moments, he carefully threw a leg over to the far side. Then he walked away that direction and regarded the wall from the other side. The other edge was rounded the same way.

Okay, if they're going to experiment with me I should experiment, too. I'll sit over here this time.

Magnus sat towards the front of the cell where the bright pane dominated the wall. The edge was highly rounded there. He rubbed his hand across it to get a feel for it.

After a minute he stood and returned to his spot against a wall. He did not have to wait long. The translucent structure wavered again.

This time the rounded shelf was constant, but the wall started short and grew in height, plateau by plateau from the front of the cell to the back. Magnus examined it carefully. The rounded edge was the same as that he had felt where he had been sitting on the previous wall… and the thickness of the wall was that of the original wall where he had chosen to sit.

Ah. When I choose a spot, they take note of the features there, then mutate it. It zeroes in on what I choose, iteration by iteration.

There was nothing else to do, so Magnus worked with the wall for some time. After selecting from many more random variations of the surface, he had guided the shape into a long force field couch, complete with back support and armrests. The new feature of his cell was reasonably comfortable, though it remained smooth and unyielding.

23

Magnus had been sitting in the new lounge trying to brainstorm escape plans when a bright window opened behind the force field in the feeding corner of his cell. A rovling slid a new plate forward. This time it held stacks of Terran food bars.

He smiled.

"Thanks! Come on in, make yourself at home," Magnus said.

He watched in shock as the rovling advanced over the plate and walked into Magnus's room.

"You understand me?" he asked, coming slowly to his feet. His heart started into high gear as he wondered what the rovling intended. Would it attack him? Or talk to him?

The rovling twitched, then wandered over toward his evolved force-field lounge.

"What do you think of that?" Magnus asked.

The rovling walked around the lounge full circle. It did not seem to pay Magnus any attention. Magnus eyed the open door it had left in the wall.

"Let's go outside now," Magnus suggested.

The rovling turned back toward the door and walked toward it. Magnus took two steps after it, then the alien artifact flashed brighter and emitted a high-pitched whining noise. Magnus regarded it in awe, caught between an impulse to dart out after the rovling or investigate the artifact.

Magnus strode over and snatched up the glowing cylinder, then headed back over toward the open door. He reached the door just behind the rovling, expecting it to close and cut him off. But the door remained open. Magnus put his hand through, verifying that the force field was down. He shuffled through rapidly.

The corridor beyond had a flat vertical wall facing his cell, and an angled one on the far side, forming the usual triangular side-space where roving tunnels joined the corridor without jutting into the main passage. There were no rovlings nearby other than the one he had followed out.

Magnus looked down the corridor. He saw four other rovling-sized doors on the same side of the corridor as his.

Those could be the doors of the other cells!

"Yat? Arakaki? Can you hear me?" he asked over his link.

"Magnus! What's going on? We can hear you clearly," Yat said.

"I've escaped my cell."

"How the hell did you manage that you cagey bastard?" Arakaki exclaimed.

"I asked a rovling to let me out," Magnus answered. He could only imagine what they would do with that answer.

What now?

He looked at the cylindrical artifact in his hands. It flashed urgently.

"What do you want?" he whispered to it. "Where are we going?"

Suddenly the rovling turned toward Magnus. It advanced, shaking its body as if highly agitated.

"What's wrong?" Magnus asked it.

"Can you open our door?" Arakaki transmitted.

"Do you have any food?" Yat added.

"I have food, but this rovling's having a fit," Magnus said. "I'm not sure how or why it listened to me, I think—"

Magnus kicked at it, sending it scuttling backward.

25

"I want to stay out here!" he said out loud.

The machine moved faster, running in an arc around him toward a wall. Another rovling appeared at the mouth of a tube across from him.

"Guys, it's going south. I have something from the dead ships out there with me, but it's operational. I think it might be helping me."

"Is it a Trilisk AI?" Arakaki asked.

I wish.

Magnus kicked at the new rovling. Two more rovlings ran down the corridor toward him. He had not seen where they came from.

"I don't think so. I don't have any weapons. More rovlings coming. Hang in there," he said.

More rovlings arrived second by second. Soon Magnus faced dozens of them. Two rovlings with sharp looking sword-arms waving before them advanced on his position. Another rovling sent a projectile into the floor beside him.

"Okay, okay, I'm going back in," he said out loud.

Magnus dropped to the floor and backed into his cell. The door shut after him.

He remained on all fours, breathing heavily.

"Yat? Arakaki?"

The connection had dropped and could not be re-established.

He held the artifact up and regarded it.

"What the hell was all that all about?" he asked.

It flickered weakly but supplied no answers.

The force field lounge shape he had created was still there. As he looked at it, a second force field wall appeared across the room.

Time to design a bed, I guess.

Chapter 6

Caden sat in the bright central room of a Celaran house in Blackhab. The windows had been closed to prevent infant Celarans from wandering in. A new generation had recently come bursting out of the vines, wriggling and gliding every which way across the entire habitat. Caden was terrified that he might accidentally hurt one. The Celaran young were only about as long as his forearm. At least the small flyers seemed to have instinctual fear of the Terrans, who must have resembled ground predators to them.

Siobhan padded out in her undersheers. She stretched her long, thin body languorously. Her outstretched arms could touch the ceiling easily. Caden caught himself staring in awe.

Siobhan laughed. "I never get tired of those looks you give me."

"I never get tired of looking."

Siobhan wandered over to stand at the window.

"So what's the standard procedure when part of the team comes back online? Are we supposed to wait at home base or go out searching for the others?" she asked.

"Well, they left us one of the *Iridar*s, so I'm guessing the latter. Still, we don't *have* to go back," Caden said. "We could go our own way."

"Quit the team?"

"If we go back… maybe we'll just die again," Caden said.

"I guess we're TMs now… we're set if we go to a Core World. But it would be boring. Let's go back out. If we die, the column will just make more of us!"

"Look, I know that the Trilisk column makes seemingly perfect copies of us, probably correct copies down to the subatomic level. But no matter how good the copy, *it's not me*. I am *this* collection of atoms and I don't want to die." Caden pointed at his head. "I'm inside here. My consciousness. It does help to know copies of me are out there, or more could be made if I die, but I'll still be dead."

"I hear you," Siobhan said. "But we *are* going to die. Even if we had Trilisk super bodies that don't age... sooner or later, somehow, someday, we'll die anyway. Life is the most precious thing I can imagine, yet I take risks all the time. I want to really enjoy what time I have."

"I felt the same, when I was younger. Now I know, *really* know, we're not invincible."

"Have you been able to catch up on everything?" Siobhan asked, changing the subject.

"I tried, but the cleaned logs they left behind for us are kind of dry. I'm hoping Telisa will fill us in on the juicy stuff they're hiding from Shiny!"

"Oh, yeah, me too, for sure. It all worked out pretty well... we're in an alliance with the Celarans! And the Quarus might be our friends someday, without any Trilisks to screw it all up."

"How about these Rovans?" Caden asked. "That's some crazy stuff. They seem kinda like big turtles with armies of crabs working for them."

"Yeah, and the rovling tunnels must be a pain in the ass, since we can barely fit through them. I've often imagined how much it would suck if we found the ruins of some physically small race with whole cities of tiny rooms we couldn't fit into."

Caden nodded. "We'd just rely upon the attendants, I guess. You're right, if that happens it just won't be the same. We'd be standing there next to a building the size of a land car, unable to go inside."

"We could VR it, I guess, and send tiny robots in hooked up to us, so we could feel like we were really in there," she said.

"Yeah, but hooking into VR on an alien planet doesn't feel safe. We could stay on the ship."

"None of it's safe, ever," she said.

Caden let the conversation pause. He still wondered what their lives would be like if they went off on their own. He supposed Siobhan would be bored to tears in a few months. Maybe he would be, too. Plus now that they were beyond famous, it would never be the same as the life he had known before.

A new connection came into his link from Cilreth.

"We got an urgent message from Telisa… our Telisa," Cilreth said.

"We're copies… maybe even copies of copies… do we really have our own Telisa anymore?" Imanol grumbled on the channel.

"Whatever. The one who asked for us to be resurrected," Cilreth said. "They've encountered an alien trap in interstellar space. The message is a request for assistance with a big warning. There's a powerful battleship there that can dampen spinners, so if we show, she says to 'show up with a big footprint or with no footprint at all.'"

"What?" Imanol asked, exasperated.

"She means, come in force or come in stealthed," Cilreth explained.

"How does she know we're here?" asked Siobhan.

"The message was general. She doesn't know Taishi got us out."

"We could ask the Space Force for a task group," Caden said.

"We could... but we're at Blackhab, and there *are* a bunch of Celaran ships around, so..." Cilreth trailed off, her point obvious.

"So stealth is definitely a possibility to consider," Caden finished for her.

"If we come in with the Space Force, there will be a big battle and our teammates might be killed," Siobhan said. "Stealth is better, especially if these Rovans are as lousy with security as they're reported to be."

"Are you guys in? Up to go save our fearless leader?" Cilreth asked.

"She's probably already dead," Imanol pointed out in typical scintillating fashion.

"We're in," Siobhan said for Caden and herself.

"I have nothing better to do. I'll come, assuming Snake isn't coming," Imanol said.

"As Imanol said, we might be too late, but we should leave soon in case we can still help," Cilreth said. "Get your things from *Iridar*... if you have anything. I'm meeting with Lee. I think she can get us stealth spheres and breaker claws at least, maybe even some of those new Rovan style force field packs."

"Let's hit it!" Siobhan said out loud to Caden excitedly. She ran back into the other room.

Caden followed more slowly. Siobhan was in their room, slipping into a new Veer suit. They had no weapons or other PIT gear other than some gliding equipment and four Celaran boost rods which were charging in the corner.

"You have anything on *Iridar*?" she asked.

"A few things. Some weapons," he said. "Unless they cleaned all of it out when we died."

"When we died. Right. Let's go check it out, then we'll meet up with the others."

Caden put on his Veer suit and the gliding equipment. Then they left the house to fly to the *Iridar* amid playful swarms of baby Celarans.

***

Caden and Siobhan drifted down toward a gray-green platform the size of a house on the inner surface of Blackhab. A forest of Celaran vines grew underneath and all around the platform. The surface gave slightly as Caden alighted upon it, even though he experienced less than half of an Earth gravity there. The Terran-adapted force field device felt heavy but reassuring on his back. He had drained a third of a lift rod's power to get here carrying the load.

Cilreth and Imanol had already arrived. They were peering into the forest that topped out about a meter below the platform.

Caden looked out over the thick vine growth that surrounded them as he folded up his glider wings. He spotted a group of ten or twelve young Celarans watching nervously from over forty meters away. They flew in tight circles around the vine stems, blindingly fast, then disappeared.

Siobhan smiled next to him. It was always a 'sunny day' in Blackhab. Several floating Celaran homes were visible in the bright sky, their confusing surfaces dotted with circular windows and entrance hatches.

An adult Celaran flew up to Cilreth. Caden's link identified the newcomer as Lee.

"Lee?" called Siobhan.

"Bright star in the sky! You've returned from the roots to fly again!" Lee replied through their links.

"Haha. It's good to see you," Siobhan said.

Caden felt out of place. He had died. The disconnect made his current reality feel like a dream or a VR session. Knowing he had been gone for a long time made him feel like it was time to get back to work, but from his perspective, he had been in combat less than a week ago.

"Are you enjoying the warm starlight, Caden? Welcome back from under the roots!" Lee said.

"I'm good, thanks!" Caden said. "Glad to see you're still around. Are any Celaran ships interested in going to help Telisa?"

"Yes! There are six ships ready to fly under the darkest leaf if we must," Lee said. The Celaran wriggled in the air energetically but barely made forward progress.

Imanol rolled his eyes. "Whoever booted Lee off the team was thinking straight, for once," Imanol said aloud. Caden was glad Lee could not sense his offline speech.

"Lee wasn't booted off!" Siobhan said. "She went to go lead her own team."

"As long as we don't have to deal with her. Two children on the team are enough," he said.

Instead of firing back with an angry retort, Siobhan just smiled.

"It's good to have you back, Imanol," she said sweetly. Imanol stared at her in horror.

Caden laughed. "Yeah. We missed our doom-n-gloom man," he said, slapping Imanol on the shoulder.

Imanol had never looked more uncomfortable.

"So what now?" he growled, changing the subject.

"Maybe we should take *Iridar* after all. It's not as stealthy as the Celaran ships, but a ship is a ship," Cilreth said.

"It would certainly be more comfortable than traveling in a Celaran melon-ship," Imanol said.

"Melon?" Caden asked.

"Yeah, you know, round, kinda hollow."

"Oh. Yeah, but won't the Terran ship give us away?" Siobhan said.

"Not if we turn down the spinner before we hit that trap zone," Cilreth said. "Then we could prepare and approach slowly, get an idea of what we're headed into."

"It might be good if the Rovans do notice it," Imanol said. "We could use it as a distraction."

"Sacrifice a Space Force ship just as a distraction?" Caden said aghast.

"Yeah. We're TMs. We can do that," Imanol said matter-of-factly. "It's not like we'd be leaving a crew behind."

Siobhan opened her mouth to protest, but Cilreth cut her off.

"We bring it. It might be an option. We won't sacrifice it unless it looks called for," Cilreth said.

She's using her in-charge voice, Caden noted to himself. *I suppose she is the senior one here.*

"Okay. That'll give us six light Celaran cruisers and a Terran assault ship," Siobhan said. "We'll show up with no footprint… plus a distraction footprint."

Chapter 7

Barrai watched a squadron of twelve ships form up and head out for the *Sharplight*. The Rovan vessels were each the size of a Terran light cruiser. The Rovan battleship itself, if indeed it was a ship and not some kind of starbase, was not moving to intercept her. That alone gave Barrai reason to hope.

If I don't have to fight that monster then I have a chance.

Dozens of ruined alien ships littered the spinner-dampened zone of space. Barrai put some of the ship's threat analysis systems on the wreckage, just in case Rovan weapons had been hidden there. So far, none of the dead hulks had proven to be hiding anything significant.

Barrai considered the wrecks. If the Rovans could use force fields against the *Sharplight*, they might try to use the hulks as kinetic weapons. She decided to move farther away from the wrecks to avoid such a possibility.

Barrai passed her programs controlling the *Sharplight* a directive to fight where she chose. The *Sharplight* charged its storage rings and accelerated away. She had altered the battle programs to anticipate and respond to force fields quickly. Barrai reserved the right to intervene and prioritize the ship's energy allocations, but for the most part, Terran reactions were too slow to direct fire.

This time, I don't have to be shy. I'll be making the first strike with the full weight of the Sharplight's firepower.

A link request came in from outside the *Sharplight*.

For a split second, Barrai thought it might be the Rovans, but the link ID said it was from Adair.

She accepted the connection.

"Don't let them see you," Barrai sent.

"I'm close enough to get this connection without being detected," Adair said.

"Then get away! Go back to where you were!"

"I came to help you! I won't hide frozen while an ally fights."

"Telisa and the others left for your position. They're relying on you to get them into the Rovan battleship."

"Impossible."

"They're out there now. Return to the expected rendezvous point."

"You have to jump ship. There's no way to break off," Adair said. "They'll board you and capture you. If you activate your stealth orb, I can pick you up."

"The plan is to turn and fight them," Barrai said. "I'm a distraction."

"No! That's exactly what they want," Adair said. "They're trying to hem you in so they can fill your ship full of rovlings!"

"Let them! I've made many improvements to this ship. We have a dozen new hardpoints and hundreds of soldier robots equipped with anti-rovling weapons."

The *Sharplight* came about and spat energy at the lead Rovan ship. It was unlikely it would hit; the enemy squadron was already performing randomized spirals to avoid energy strikes from many light seconds out.

"It won't be enough," Adair said.

"I don't have the energy to keep breaking through their blocking fields and shoot their ships at the same time. I have no other choice. At least this way, I can take out an army of rovlings."

"I'll sneak in behind them," Adair said.

"No! The *Iridar* can't withstand those weapons. Stay cloaked, find the others, and assist them in the rescue operation!"

Barrai closed the channel. She had made her case; who knew if the Terran AI would listen to her? Right now, she had other plans.

Every one of those ships I kill will mean less rovlings later.

The *Sharplight* recycled the rings dedicated to heavy weapons and fired again.

Barrai rode a wave of adrenaline watching the tactical. She had done this thousands of times in VR simulations but this was *real*. And the near inevitable result would be another rovling incursion like the one she had barely survived.

A part of her noted that if the Rovans were to decide they only wanted to destroy the *Sharplight* rather than board it, they would succeed. There were too many ships and their shields were too strong.

You're getting closer now... I'll punish you for that.

The light from a Rovan ship's explosion reached *Sharplight*, accentuating her point.

The *Sharplight* shuddered as it ran up against an invisible barrier at an acute angle. Instead of shooting or ramming through it, Barrai accelerated along its face and then turned with the barrier at the keel of the ship. Her maneuver proved sound; no Rovan energy beams connected with the ship.

She directed her HEW cruiser to face the enemy. As it came about, she released another full barrage at a Rovan ship. The ship rolled away the next few seconds, taking about half the energy she had dished out. Barrai cursed.

Suddenly new objects appeared on her space combat tactical: A swarm of missiles headed into the ship she had weakened.

"Dammit Adair! I told you to get the hell out of here," Barrai said aloud, but she watched the missiles in anticipation all the same. The targeted Rovan ship tried to run.

Barrai overrode her programs to fire a weak pulse before the *Sharplight* was ready for another alpha strike, trying to ding the Rovan ship if it took the optimal course to avoid the missiles. Seconds passed before she would be able to tell what happened.

"C'mon, C'mon, get it…"

Her strike raked the ship. It slowed, then the missiles came in. It exploded.

She exulted for only a moment; eight of the ten remaining Rovan ships were almost close enough to launch their own missiles. Two others had diverted from *Sharplight* to attempt to search for the enemy they probably could not detect. Barrai had not wanted the help at the cost of Telisa's mission, all the same, she knew this improved her chances of victory… or at least survival.

Energy beams drained half her shield power away. Barrai knew it was not intended to kill her. The ships were ganging up to keep her energy reserves low. They wanted her to divert energy to recharge the shields instead of run or fire back. The *Sharplight* shuddered again as they tried to pin her down.

Barrai looked at her energy systems. She still had enough for a full round of point defense when the inevitable launch came. She shaved off twenty percent of that to get to her full strike earlier, since no missiles were yet in flight against her. She fired at the nearest Rovan ship.

I love high energy weapons, but sometimes it would be nice to have just one full launch of missiles.

Barrai felt that Adair had likely bugged out after dropping the batch of missiles. Despite the help, Barrai was angry at the Terran AI for letting the Rovans know it was out there. That would just make Telisa's rescue mission that much more difficult.

The eight Rovan ships coming after her launched a mass of missiles. Two seconds after that, one of the ships exploded as *Sharplight*'s last strike cut into it.

The *Sharplight* automatically took stock of the threat. The sensors verified that the missiles were incursion modules. Barrai let it run the numbers. The Space Force ship could not possibly stop them all, but the new calculations for point defense allocation left her enough energy to strike again. The *Sharplight* fired at another Rovan cruiser.

Barrai's algorithms showed that it was no use to try and run. Force fields were out there ready to block any escape, and the seven ships were turning away to await the outcome of their incursion salvo. One of *Sharplight*'s primary emitters found the energy to fire, destroying two incoming missiles with one shot. Somehow the Rovan cruiser she had targeted managed to endure her last offensive salvo.

The rest of the energy went into the shields and topped off the energy rings she would need for the laser emplacements. Her point defenses were charged and ready.

Barrai still felt angry. She paced for a minute, waiting for the missiles.

Is Adair gone? Or might it have come back to shoot at these missiles with me?

Barrai did not know which one to hope for. The missiles arrived.

She watched her point defenses butcher half the incursion modules. The energy each emitter had used was sufficient: each shot killed its target. She gladly accepted the small victory.

The *Sharplight* shuddered from multiple impacts.

It was time.

Barrai took one last look at the external tactical. The *Sharplight* continued to maneuver, though sluggishly. The seven surviving Rovan ships regrouped with the two that had broken off to search for Adair. They would probably wait to see if the boarding force could cut up the ship from the inside.

There was no sign of Adair or the *Iridar*. Apparently the Terran AI had decided to take her suggestion, though it could not resist one launch at the Rovans on the way out.

Red marks appeared across the internal tactical as the *Sharplight* reported breaches all over the ship. Dozens of incursion modules had made it through.

Barrai smiled. Most of the breach points were in the expected locations.

Now the fight gets more personal. Just the way I like it.

Chapter 8

Arakaki's stomach grumbled for the thousandth time. She decided she had endured enough; Arakaki told her Veer suit to block the signals. It injected her with something and the hunger went away.

She opened her eyes a little. Across the dull gray floor, Yat dozed upon a translucent blue force field. Stubble darkened his face. Arakaki looked at his disheveled hair and the look of pain on his face.

We can't give up.

She pushed her torso up with her arms, slipped one leg under the other and smoothly regained her feet. She walked over to their shared force field toilet area in one corner.

If our waste can get out, why can't we? If we can fool it somehow. Maybe by taking our Veer suits off?

Yat got up without uttering a word and started to examine the cell with her.

"I thought we agreed you would stick to trying to hack the door with your link and I would cover the physical side," Arakaki said.

"We have enough time for each of us to do both," Yat pointed out. "Besides, I'm stuck. Our links weren't built to communicate with random alien electronics."

"Magnus said he had food. Did he figure something out about his cell that we haven't?" Arakaki asked.

"I suppose it's possible," Yat said, his voice a dirge. "I think maybe he got some food when he escaped, though. Or maybe we misunderstood him. Maybe he was saying he *needed* food."

They visited every inch of their cell, looking carefully for any overlooked detail, tapping the force field, and racking their brains.

Movement in Arakaki's peripheral vision caught her attention. She turned to watch a corner of their cell. A window of light grew upward from the floor.

"Heads up!" Arakaki snapped. She pointed.

Yat turned and saw it. He grabbed his stun baton.

Arakaki grabbed her own baton while feverishly hoping that it was Magnus breaking them out of their prison.

A rovling scuttled into the cell. Then another. Yat and Arakaki retreated to the far side of the force field seat they had created.

More rovlings came in. Arakaki guessed there were ten or more. The alien machines flanked their position. Arakaki did not swing.

"What could they want? Is this it?" Yat asked.

Arakaki just waited, her back against Yat's. Their equipment had been drained from the last fight before their capture. Even their stun batons were merely clubs now.

The rovlings completed the encirclement, then moved in.

Why did they keep us here if they meant to kill us all along?

They both started swinging at the dog-sized machines. Arakaki damaged one with her club and kicked another, but three others grabbed her legs. She lost her balance.

Yat turned toward her.

"No!" he yelled. He kicked one rovling away from her. Three more took its place. He lifted his baton to crush one, grunting with the effort. Rovlings pulled him from behind, sending him reeling backward.

Arakaki thrust her baton into the body of a rovling, but the glancing blow did little harm. The machines started to drag her toward the opening of the cell.

From the ground, Arakaki looked over her shoulder. As the machines dragged her away, they cornered Yat on the opposite end of the cell.

"Arakaki! Hang on!" he said, swinging furiously. The rovlings darted back to avoid his attack, then charged back in to pin him.

They only want me.

Arakaki's back was lifted from the floor. She pinned her legs against the door, bringing herself to a halt. She grabbed her baton with both hands and struggled to free it from the rovling that held it. Just as she almost wrested control of the rod from her assailant, rovlings pushed her feet toward each other and she slipped through the opening. Another two rovlings pulled the rod from her grasp.

The sounds of Yat's fighting faded as they dragged her into a corridor outside the cell.

Arakaki kept fighting. Her arms were not strong enough to break free or even flex more than ten or twenty degrees. She brought her legs up in sudden surges and tried to kick the rovlings away. She managed to knock one free after several tries, but the efforts tired her.

They took her to the end of the corridor and around a corner.

Arakaki coiled her body. Her abdominals were strong enough to drag the rovlings along the floor. She reached a near-fetal position, then kicked again with both her feet together. A rovling limped away with a broken leg. It was replaced by another.

She compressed and kicked several times. The rovlings adjusted their holds each time until they found spots from which she could not break them loose. Her link added the new corridor to its internal map of the ship it had started when they were first brought to their prison.

"Yat? Magnus? Anyone?" she transmitted.

Finally the rovlings turned at a door and dragged her into a new room. Arakaki half expected to see a Rovan, but the room only held machines. She saw silver cylinders against a wall connected with pipes. Complex machines stood between flat tables or platforms with rows of corded tools beyond them. Two rovling tubes emptied into the room near the floor under a Rovan-style storage cabinet like they had seen in the bunker on their earlier expedition.

They pulled and pushed her to a sterile white platform. It looked like an autosurgery mat.

The rovlings dragged her up and slid her across it.

Dissection? No!

Arakaki told her Veer suit to give her all it had. She howled as new energy flowed into her.

"Frag you bastards to hell!" she yelled. She kicked one rovling away, then another. Her hand pulled out a combat blade from a sheath at her hip. The weapon was not ideal for rovlings, but that did not stop her from driving it straight into the thorax of the nearest octoped.

The knife stuck in the rovling, refusing to come out, so Arakaki used it as a handle to swing the machine across her body and smash it into another rovling. She felt a tweak in her bicep tendon as she overstrained it with her new strength. There was no pain, so she ignored it. She tried to roll away, but too many enemies secured her from all angles.

She heard her ragged gasps for air taking more time between her desperate curses. She floundered in lactic acid burn and oxygen debt.

The rovlings dragged Arakaki to the center of the platform. She thrashed against the rovlings weakly. She managed to lift one rovling up with her right arm until another roving piled on and dragged her limb back.

Dots started to dance before her eyes and she felt light headed. Her face was wet.

"I will kill every last one of you," she growled, then her world faded to black.

***

Arakaki's back felt cold. She took a deep breath, then bolted awake as memory came charging back into her consciousness.

"Yat!" she snapped.

There was no answer. Her Veer suit had been removed, exposing her skin to the cool, dry air of the lab. Her undersheers gave her only a thin layer of protection over her torso and hips. Arakaki crossed her arms over her chest defensively.

There were no rovlings in sight. She flexed her legs. She seemed intact, so she slid off the platform and looked for blood. Everything was clean.

They must have examined me. Or tested me. Yuck.

She felt herself for cuts or soreness. Again, nothing.

"Where did you go?" she said to herself. Her voice sounded cowed. That made her angry at herself as well as the rovlings.

Damn little tentacle-munching paste heads.

She slid down from the platform. The floor felt cool to her bare feet. In a Veer suit, she seldom felt hot or cold—unless she was being hit by a laser—and such details were never noted. Now she felt vulnerable.

A low shelf across the room caught her attention. It had Terran items arrayed across it.

Her suit and weapons.

Arakaki snatched up her suit and slipped into it in record time. Then she grabbed a PAW. It had no projectile rounds left, but somehow it had been recharged. Arakaki accepted that gratefully. At least she had a beam weapon.

She grabbed her knife and her stun baton from the shelf. The stun baton had also been charged.

Is this their apology for dragging me in here kicking and screaming? Not good enough.

Arakaki looked the direction from which they had dragged her in. Should she return to find Yat? Or would that just cause her to be imprisoned again?

She decided to investigate the rest of the lab first, then head back the way they had dragged her. She saw an open door at the other end of the room.

Arakaki slipped between a large machine and another platform to get to another walkway in the room. The walkway was a solid metal or ceramic with tiny ridges giving it traction. She checked the ceiling for rovlings or any signs of weapons emplacements, but saw nothing. Arakaki held her PAW before her and advanced down the walkway to see the next room.

She walked through the doorway and stopped short: a huge shelled creature stood two meters before her.

The creature's coloration surprised her: the shell and limbs were aqua blue, but the head—At least, the part of it that jutted forward from the shell with four eyes and a scythe-like mouth—was a dull orange.

A damn Rovan.

Arakaki's PAW snapped up. Her mouth set in a grimace.

"What have you done to me, you paste-brained incomalcon?"

Internally, Arakaki acknowledged that her choice of words was probably not ideal for first contact with an alien race, but she was in no mood for friendly hellos.

The Rovan made no move to defend itself. Its head turned slightly until she stood directly between the front two beady eyes. It made some kind of huffing noise that she supposed might be audio speech, then its reply came through her link.

"Terran calm -Rovan appears- Terran brandishes weapons."

"Damn right I do. After you've tossed me in your cell, starved me, dragged me out and attacked me with your rovlings. *Did you cut me open?*"

The Rovan did not answer immediately, so Arakaki changed her demand.

"Take me to my friends. Or bring them to me."

"Terran demands course of action -Rovan accepts- situation upgrade? Terran demands course of action -Rovan refuses- situation degrades?"

Arakaki kept herself on a razor's edge of alertness. There was no sound of any rovling scuttling about nearby. Nothing moved in her peripheral vision.

"Terran demands course of action, correct. If you accept... Rovan accepts, Rovan lives. That's an upgrade."

The Rovan's shell looked wet. Arakaki decided it was simply highly polished. The eyes were creepy, but more similar to Terran eyes than Vovokan or Celaran eyes in that they had a discernible pupil.

Arakaki wanted to walk to her right and put her back against the wall, but then she wondered what might happen if the Rovan simply charged forward. She would be crushed by that immense shell, or cleaved by those scythe-like mandibles.

"Terran demands course of action -Rovan refuses- situation degrades?" repeated the Rovan.

"Take me to the others. Release us all."

"Rovan controls Terran -Terran emits threats- Rovan controls Terran."

"Release us or I'll shoot you and go find my friends myself."

Does it have a force shield? Of course it does. That's why it let me have my weapons. I'm not a threat.

Arakaki shifted her weapon slightly. Her bicep tendon felt normal.

Wait a second! I'm sure I tore or even ruptured it... did they repair me? Or... this is not real!

Arakaki digested her revelation. She was in virtual reality, though her link had no idea. It must have been hacked—which might have been easy for a Vovokan, but seemed impossible for a Rovan—or else it had been removed and replaced with a new one.

The thought filled her with despair. Arakaki avoided the turmoil and focused on her current problem.

I can't really hurt it. It just wants to know if I'll shoot.

Arakaki lowered her weapon.

"I can't force you to release me. But if you don't, you'll never be friends with our civilization. And there are more than just us. We've made allies of other advanced life forms, too."

"Terran agitated -Rovan ignores threats- Terran returns to negotiation."

"I may not be able to defend myself, but my civilization can, if you plan aggression."

The Rovan's head dropped a few centimeters. Arakaki could not interpret the motion.

"Terran agitated -Rovan concludes experiment- Terran forgets."

Arakaki's world slipped away.

Michael McCloskey

Chapter 9

Maxsym listened to the sound of his breathing to calm himself as he drifted through empty darkness. The vague figures of his cloaked teammates were green squiggles in the distance.

How did I get here? I'm supposed to be a scientist, not an adventurer.

Despite the complaints in his internal monologue, Maxsym often marveled at how lucky he was to have the opportunity to examine aliens that no Terran had yet encountered. He would just rather be studying them than fighting their robotic armies.

"Rovlings," Telisa transmitted.

Maxsym saw enemies light up on the shared tactical.

"How did they detect us?" Marcant asked.

"I don't think they did. They're on those dead ships," Telisa said.

"What are they doing?" Marcant wondered. "Those vessels don't look Rovan."

"Do not engage. We have to slip through to Adair and the *Iridar*," Telisa said firmly.

Maxsym needed no such orders. He was not about to get the attention of a rovling swarm.

Telisa led them through a cluster of the ships. Maxsym saw broken silver and maroon hulls. Most of the destroyer-sized ships were fairly flat with sharpened ends, but he saw three rounder shapes among them. Their surfaces held spiral depressions that made them look like works of art.

One of his attendants scanned a distant ship. Maxsym checked its feed. Rovlings crawled over half of a dead hulk like ants harvesting a broken melon. Maxsym wondered what fate had befallen the ship's owners.

"*Sharplight* came upon this group of ships in the interstellar void just as the others did. Now, floating through local space in our suits, we come right up to these ships? What's going on?" Marcant asked.

"It was me who routed us by this group of ships. I wanted to see them," Telisa explained.

Of course. She brought us closer to them on purpose. Her curiosity is unquenchable, Maxsym thought.

"And what about this entire area?" Maxsym asked. "It's still a tiny target to hit out between the stars."

"Adair said it was a trap. That implies that they brought down our spinner, at least," Marcant said. "Let's hope they did not somehow control our navigation, as well."

We're always in over our heads, Maxsym thought. *It must be inevitable when dealing with technologically superior civilizations… even dead ones.*

"Another ship ahead. A small Rovan one," Telisa transmitted.

Maxsym referenced the tactical and looked for himself. His attendants helped him view it from their position many kilometers out.

"Some kind of local rovling transport, I bet," Marcant said. "It's too small to be anything more significant."

"It could be some kind of scout or fighter," Telisa said. Maxsym thought she was merely trying on different ideas for size. He liked Marcant's explanation. The ship was long and slender, with hatches on either side to the fore and another large one aft.

"Well the rovlings had to get out here somehow," Marcant pointed out. "They can't navigate in space like our attendants do."

"It's a good guess," Telisa conceded. "They could have been dropped off by something else, but that does look like a rovling delivery vehicle, doesn't it? Light, unarmed and a lot of hatches to load and unload them quickly."

"Maybe we could commandeer it," Maxsym suggested.

"Maybe," Telisa said. "It might be useful for getting into that battleship," she said.

It would sure beat floating around out here in our space suits.

Telisa altered her vector slightly. The others followed suit. Maxsym saw that their new course would bring them even closer to the little ship.

"Marcant, do you think you could get it to open? To fly us away?" Telisa asked.

"Open, yes. Fly away, maybe. But I think the rovlings would notice. And if they tell the battleship, it might know something is afoot."

"Then they might just open fire on it," Maxsym said. "We'd be sitting ducks."

"What's a sitting duck?" Marcant asked.

"Something we don't want to be," Maxsym answered.

A connection from Adair came to Maxsym's link.

"This is Adair. I'm behind you," the AI transmitted. The *Iridar* appeared on Maxsym's view of the tactical.

"You moved from your spot?" demanded Telisa.

"I went to help Barrai," Adair said. "I managed to kill one Rovan ship, but she still has several attackers."

"Any idea how it will play out? And how long it might take?" Telisa asked.

"The *Sharplight* has been heavily engaged. I suspect it will also be boarded," Adair said. "It could take hours."

"We had a big fight with a rovling army," Marcant said. "Barrai has made a lot of improvements to *Sharplight* since then."

"Then maybe she can last several hours," Adair said.

"Her improvements were major," Telisa said.

"Okay, but did the army you fought come from a battleship like that?" Adair asked.

The question felt rhetorical. No one answered.

Point taken, Maxsym thought. *Barrai might face even more rovlings than we survived last time.*

"Everyone get aboard," Telisa said. "Barrai is keeping the Rovans distracted and we need to use this time wisely."

The *Iridar* had matched their course, so it was easy for Maxsym's attendants to slowly accelerate him toward their cloaked ship.

Maxsym found himself wondering if the others were still alive as he neared the *Iridar*. He imagined Magnus and Arakaki, tough and experienced, fighting the rovling swarm that caught them by surprise. If the rovlings captured them, what would they do? The obvious answers were rip them to shreds, or take them back to the battleship. Once there they would be studied and interrogated, at least if the battleship had living Rovans or a Rovan AI aboard.

A ship that size would definitely have a smart brain controlling it. Unless the Rovans just didn't make AIs.

By the time Maxsym and Marcant landed on the shuttle deck, Telisa had already emerged from her space suit. The bay was much smaller than the *Sharplight*'s, but Maxsym immediately felt at home. He queued up some of his experiment results from the local computing resources, just in case Telisa gave him time to review their progress.

"Charge your cloaking devices. We may only be here for minutes," Telisa said. She pointed. Maxsym brought his cloaking device to the indicated charging station in the wall.

Telisa wasted no time.

"Adair, you've watched ships return before, correct?"

"Yes."

"We'll need to consider how they come back. How quickly they travel, where do they come to station outside the battleship's protective fields, and how quickly they move inside. Did they return to the same hangars they sortied from?"

"That last, I don't know. It would be reasonable for undamaged ships to return to the same hangars. Damaged ones might well return to different ones for repairs."

"Good thought. We should snug up to ships that aren't damaged, if there are any. We need an educated guess about where to wait, and when to jump over."

"If their screens are still up, we won't be able to get onto the hulls," Maxsym pointed out.

"If that squadron engaging Barrai is victorious, they likely won't have shields up when they come back," Marcant said.

"We'll see. I don't want to wait that long... What can we do if they keep them up?" Telisa said.

"I don't know," Adair said.

Maxsym felt uncomfortable about the shields on the Rovan ships. If the team approached too quickly, a force field could kill them, and if a shield came up unexpectedly it could crush them. Terran shields were more forgiving: though they absorbed incoming electromagnetic energy in a straightforward way, they deflected kinetic attacks more than solidly stopping them. An activating Terran shield would displace someone nearby rather than crushing them outright.

"If we could get into that rovling carrier outside, maybe we could sneak in that way," Maxsym suggested.

Telisa frowned. She glanced at Maxsym.

Is she wondering if she should tell me to stay here? Or just thinking over the plan?

She seemed to make a decision.

"The rovling transport is plan B. Charge what you can. We need to keep tabs on comings and goings so we can take advantage of them. Adair, can you get us closer to the battleship without being spotted?" Telisa asked Adair.

"Probably. No guarantees. The ship has some weak shielding up all the time. You would have to get through that, then inside."

"If we can't make our way in immediately, we'll slip though when the ships that harassed Barrai return, assuming she leaves any alive."

"I feel that the *Sharplight* is outmatched," Adair said. "If not from the rovlings, just from the ranged weapons of the squadron that came out to intercept it."

Telisa's fists clenched. She paced with new energy.

"This is so frustrating. Barrai is laying her life on the line to buy us time to make this rescue happen."

"Well, it's not like we had a choice. As soon as we arrived the Rovans attacked," Marcant said.

Maxsym's thoughts returned to the rovling carrier.

"New idea," he said. He had Telisa's eager attention.

"We go sneak into that transport. Then Adair sends a missile into whatever hulk the rovlings are searching at the moment. Blow that dead ship to pieces along with the rovlings. Then, the transport ship will either return empty on its own, or maybe the battleship will send some ships out to respond. Either way, we'll have a chance to hitch a ride."

Telisa smiled. "I like it. It's risky, but we'll have a couple of chances to abort if it looks like it's going wrong."

"The strike will inform the battleship that *Iridar* is out here," Adair said.

"Maybe. Or maybe it will think it was a trap from one of the dead ships, or some last resistance from something automated," Marcant offered.

"We don't know enough about their enemy," Telisa said. "But it's worth a try."

"Are we going in our suits?" Maxsym asked, careful to hide his anxiety.

"We'll take a shuttle," Telisa said. "We can carry the missile, too. That should give Adair time to take the *Iridar* safely away before we cause a stir."

"Perhaps this mission is a bit hasty," Adair said. "How are you going to rescue anyone from that ship?"

"I won't sit by and wait while our teammates may be struggling to survive in there," Telisa said. "You don't think for a second that Magnus and Arakaki would hesitate if it were us in there?"

They would rescue me. Anyone on the PIT team would.

He used that knowledge to clear his head and prepare himself for what was to come.

Chapter 10

Magnus awakened on his rough bed-form. He had managed to choose a solid shape that let him sleep on his back in the middle with a low neck support, or lay on his sides on the edges with higher head supports. The shape choose-and-mutate system was interesting, but it could be tedious to work through to anything complex. So far, there had been no variations in softness. Whatever he got was always unyielding. Magnus supposed that creatures that lived their lives inside hard shells probably did not value soft beds.

He looked across the room.

His wide chair had been copied six times. Each one was now a different hue.

"More choices for the prisoner. Such luxury," Magnus said aloud.

He checked the cell first to make sure nothing else had changed. Then he chose a light green chair and sat on it. The other chairs faded away.

Magnus thought about the ruined hulks outside that he assumed had been destroyed by this battleship. Were those crews imprisoned like himself? The battles might have happened hundreds of years ago. Maybe those crews had died in cells like this...

To Magnus's extreme surprise, he *knew* the answer. *No.*

A link memory offered itself up. Magnus automatically accessed it.

A squadron of forty alien ships traveled through space. Magnus could see each gleaming, inscribed hull perfectly. Inside each, a massive alien brain lived out its entire life.

These were cyborg ships holding creatures that had long forgotten what it was like to live on a planet's surface under the light of a star.

Each one of those creatures had died when its hull was cracked open.

Magnus snapped back to reality as the memory ended.

"Damn, how is it possible?" he whispered. He looked over at the glowing artifact. Had it…?

It must have put this memory into my link. Those ships out there were the artificial bodies of such creatures. Its creators.

Magnus searched for other memories. Nothing new came to mind. Perhaps he could not discover new memories on demand; he might have to stumble upon them by thinking of something associated to each one.

Why did they come here?

No memories came forward to answer Magnus's question.

What did they want?

No memories. Magnus struggled to learn more. What did he need to think of?

What do you want now?

A memory came forward. At first, Magnus thought it was his experience out in the corridor during his brief escape. Then it became clear the memory was colored with more information.

The rovling had entered his room. Magnus had suspected nothing. Just playing around, he had pretended to invite it inside.

Then the rovling had been fooled. It had been reprogrammed by the artifact… something relatively easy to do given the Rovans' general lack of security features.

Magnus had been allowed to leave the cell only because the rovling was not itself. Everything was going fine as he communicated with his teammates, and then... the rovling had been updated from a Rovan control source. Its suborned program was repaired. The machine immediately called for assistance and herded Magnus back into his cell.

So that's what happened, Magnus thought. *But why is that memory enhanced?*

No answers came. But Magnus guessed it was to let him know that he could do it again.

So I can get out of here... but the rovling will fall from my control at some point...

Magnus grabbed the alien artifact and held it in his palm. He resolved to wait for a rovling to come with his food and try another escape. He wondered if it would be the same machine. Would it have learned from last time?

Such thoughts naturally led to what he would do if he succeeded.

Well, if nothing else, I need to tell the others. Try to get them out. Failing that, do I try and escape to get help?

Magnus played such a scenario out in his head. Theoretically, his artifact could be the key that would allow Marcant and Adair to really take off on their understanding of Rovan tech. Maybe they could even learn enough to reprogram all the rovlings at once...

But Yat and Arakaki sounded like they were being starved.

A rattling sound alerted him to the arrival of a rovling. The wall rose behind the force field in his feeding corner. A flat plate slid inside with bars of food. A rovling stepped halfway inside and regarded Magnus for a moment with the black eye-plates atop its flat, oval body.

"Hi. Just step back a little, there. I need to get out," Magnus said.

The Rovan machine hesitated, then it retreated back outside. Magnus crawled through after it. He stood in the outside hallway. There were no other rovlings visible.

The rovling waited within a few meters of him.

If I don't try something different, the same thing will happen again...

"Go away. Get out of here, go do something else," Magnus said.

The rovling turned and scuttled away dutifully.

Magnus looked either direction. On his right, the corridor continued only a short distance before turning right, but the corridor went on much longer on his left. Along the left stretch, he saw other portals like the one behind him.

This way.

"Yat? Jamie? I'm out again."

"Magnus!" Yat responded. "The rovlings took her out! We fought them, but she got dragged away!"

Magnus started to run forward down the corridor.

"How long ago? Any idea which way they went?"

"Over an hour I think. We were too hungry to fight very well. I have no idea where they went. Just go find her! Or get me out and let me help find her! Who knows what they're doing to her right now!"

"On it," he said.

A rovling came out of a tube a few meters ahead of him.

"Come here," Magnus said, slowing to a stop. "Open that door."

He pointed at the next door from his own. The rovling walked over to the door, then stopped. The door did not rise.

"Open it," Magnus insisted. Nothing happened.

Magnus struggled to understand what he was doing wrong. Then he became aware that his time must be running out.

"Leave now!" he commanded. The octoped skittered away.

Magnus sighed.

Can the rulers of this ship see me? Surely there are sensors around here? There has to be some kind of brain in charge of this place.

"Door, open," Magnus said. Nothing happened. He looked at the artifact in his hand.

I need you to hack the door now, not a rovling.

"Artifact, can you hack the door to open? My friend is trapped in there," Magnus said aloud.

Once again, nothing changed.

"I can't get these cell doors to open right now. I'm going to go find her!" Magnus told Yat.

"Good luck, Magnus!"

He could hear it in Yat's voice, even though that voice was only in his head. Yat wanted to beg him to do whatever it took to save her.

I will save her, he assured himself.

He examined the corridor. The rovlings could have taken her either direction. Magnus wondered if he would have heard them if they went by his cell. He was unsure how much sound insulation there was.

"Yat, can you hear me?" Magnus yelled aloud.

There was no answer.

Okay, two directions to choose from, then.

On instinct, Magnus chose the direction heading away from his cell. He took three steps, then a rovling emerged from a pipe four meters ahead of him.

"Lead me to the one you took," he told the rovling. It paused, turning to face him, then froze. Magnus cursed under his breath.

"Go," Magnus said. "Go away now!"

The rovling darted away down the corridor and into a tube.

He held up his artifact and watched it.

"Which way?" he asked it aloud. He held up the device and turned full circle. The device pulsed as it faced the corridor ahead, so Magnus kept going.

The corridor turned right. Magnus kept going. A rovling came out of a tube and headed across the corridor until it saw him, then it approached.

"Go away!" Magnus said. The rovling went back the way it came.

Magnus resumed his exploration.

He walked up to a set of doors, one on each side of the corridor. The artifact gave no reaction, so he continued. He passed a set of three rovling tubes, then the device in his hand pulsed again.

Magnus examined the corridor. He saw a panel on the surface on his left, in the triangular space of the alcove. The device pulsed again.

He realized that the panel slid upward like the lid of a Rovan storage bin. He pushed the barrier upward, revealing a vertical shaft beyond.

"What's that thing?" Magnus asked himself quietly. He held the artifact into the cylindrical shaft. It glowed brightly.

Magnus moved the artifact up and down. It quickly started to glow only when it was moving up.

"You've got to be kidding me," Magnus said. The shaft had no rungs or handles. Magnus leaned in and looked closer. He saw that the walls of the vertical tunnel were not completely smooth; there were the tiny ridges rovlings used to gain purchase on walls and ceilings.

Magnus sighed.

For Arakaki. Sure I'll do it.

Magnus took one last look around the corridor. He saw no activity, so he pocketed the artifact and then slid into the tunnel feet first. He fit inside, though not comfortably. He was able to use his legs to brace himself and keep from falling.

He conducted some experiments to see how he could move inside the tunnel. The friction between his Veer suit and the surface of the shaft was pretty high. He pushed his torso upward by pushing his knees against the side of the shaft. Then he spread his arms to hold himself, relaxed his knees and pulled them up.

Magnus sighed.

Progress. Slow progress.

Magnus pushed and pulled his way up. The process was frustratingly slow, but once he committed himself to it, it was tolerable. Within ten minutes he came to another panel which he assumed was an exit to another deck. He braced himself and checked the glowing cylinder.

"Here, huh? Okay."

Magnus forced up the rolling panel and looked out. The new deck looked the same as the old one: white corridors with alcoves sloping outward to the floor with rovling pipe exits and the occasional thick red band encircling the tunnel. Magnus wondered again why the red bands where there. The Rovans appeared to have had four eyes atop their heads, one on each corner, so it did not seem that the bands would be needed to aid with depth perception. He supposed it might be for the rovlings and not the Rovans, but had no idea why.

He crawled out, stretched his legs, and hurried on, guided by the artifact. He went left down the corridor and took a right at an intersection. Then he was directed down a smaller side tunnel and came into a large round room with a huge silvery column in the center.

Magnus looked up. The massive column rose at least a hundred meters from his position. He walked around it, but there were no doors or rovling tubes. It was not a Trilisk column, at least not like any he had seen.

Power plant? Alien gravity spinner? Superweapon?

Magnus hesitated. Whatever it was, it was important. Should he sabotage it?

I'm supposed to be saving my teammates, not destroying this ship. We don't want anything to do with this place.

Suddenly Magnus realized the artifact had led him astray. It was not showing him where Arakaki was. It was showing him the weaknesses of its enemy.

"This isn't where Arakaki is," Magnus stated. The cylinder flickered brightly several times, then went dark.

Dammit. I followed this thing all this way and Arakaki probably isn't far from that cell.

Magnus turned around.

"I'm not here to destroy the Rovans. I'm just trying to save my friends," Magnus told the artifact in case it could understand him. Then he put the small cylinder into a pocket of his Veer suit.

Magnus hurried back to the shaft and slipped back into it. He grimaced.

At least it will be easier going down... I think.

He shuffled downward. He thought about what might have happened to Arakaki while he had been on the deck above. He tried to go faster but it just tripped him up.

He left the vertical tunnel at the deck he had come from. Magnus stood in the corridor, trying to decide which way to go.

If they took her to the left, and didn't drag her down a rovling tunnel, then there's a fair chance they came this way...

Magnus headed into new territory, down the corridor past the vertical shaft. He saw more rovling tubes, but there were no clues on the floors or walls. He supposed if Arakaki had dropped something for them to find a rovling might well have picked it up. They were probably programmed to keep the place neat and clean.

He paused at the next Rovan-sized portal and examined the floor. He searched for blood, scuff marks, or dirt—anything at all that might indicate a captive had been dragged in.

Magnus was desperate. He decided to broadcast a message.

"Arakaki? Can you hear me?" he transmitted.

Magnus was shocked to get an immediate response.

"Error: Link External. Address recognized but has been uninstalled. Metadata has no forwarding address. New hardware lookup has failed. Please update your contact record with Jamie Arakaki's new hardware information and resend."

Magnus stood stunned. Arakaki's link was no longer in her head.

If Arakaki still had a head.

Chapter 11

Barrai stood ramrod straight in a metal cupola beside the top of a ramp, brandishing a missile launcher. Twenty meters before her, a laser emplacement watched over an atrium that led to the *Sharplight*'s spinner assembly. The new atrium had been a series of four or five nonessential rooms, but after the first major rovling assault, the walls had never been rebuilt.

Barrai was fine with the wide open space. Her weapon was designed to launch tiny missiles from four tubes. Each missile could destroy at least five rovlings in a straight line, detonating on the first one or two directly and sending sharp fragments flying on to destroy more. She planned to use the launcher to wipe out the first hundred or so rovlings to charge down the corridor joining the far side of the atrium.

Another missile launcher and a second Rovan pack waited at her feet, guarded by the carbon and steel walls of the cupola.

When the first rovlings appeared, she snapped her force screen on and observed them through her weapon's sights. The laser emplacement effortlessly slagged the first few, until the rovlings sensed the resistance and gathered en masse outside of its arc of fire. Barrai held her fire for the rush. Given the huge numbers of invading rovlings, each of her missiles had to count.

Circular pieces of the far walls dropped to the floor as the rovlings beyond cut themselves new passages into the area. Barrai stretched her neck as if preparing for a sparring match.

Dozens of rovlings poured out of the far corridors and the new holes in the wall. The laser emplacement started to mow them down, but it could not keep up.

Barrai opened fire.

Fooooosh! Foooosh! Ba-Boom-Boom!

Smoke obscured the corridor. At first, Barrai simply thought the devastation she had visited upon the enemy had stirred up a cloud of debris. In the next few moments, it became clear the cloud was not dissipating. Barrai understood what was happening: it was a defensive countermeasure.

So they have some tricks up their sleeves as well. Little bastards.

Barrai quickly told the *Sharplight* to step up atmospheric processing in the area to clear the smoke. Then she flicked through several light frequencies, looking for ways to defeat the smoke while the laser emplacement fired blindly. Barrai consoled herself knowing that there were probably so many rovlings that the laser would still hit many. With that thought, she added her own firepower to the corridor ahead despite the lack of vision.

Fooooosh! Foooosh! Ba-Boom! Boom!

A rain of projectiles rose from the gloom below, focusing on the laser emplacement. Barrai wondered if the rovlings could actually see through the haze, or if they had simply mapped the position of the emplacement earlier and knew exactly where it was.

Either way, the fate of the emplacement was sealed. It resisted several dozen rounds, but the surface abraded quickly. Barrai thought many of the rounds hitting the emplacement were coming from the right flank, far from the corridor.

I've cleared the corridor with missiles twice, but the ones that came out of the holes have massed on the right.

Barrai swung her weapon right and unleashed another barrage.

Fooooosh! Foooosh! Boom! Foooosh! Boom! Boom!

The *Sharplight* finally caught up to the smoke and started to clear it. Movement became visible below among a field of debris. The laser emplacement had been silenced.

Barrai took stock of the local battle from her vantage point. In another few seconds she saw that the atrium was a sea of rovlings. The rapid-firing laser was the main thing that had been holding them back. Fresh waves entered from the far side. Special models wandered among the others, doubtless capable of powerful explosions or other forms of destruction. It looked certain the battle was lost, again.

Barrai called out her reinforcements and launched the last missile from her first launcher at the densest group she saw.

Foooosh! Boom!

A Terran battle sphere, modeled after its Vovokan predecessors, floated out of a passage below her cupola and opened fire.

Kzap, kzap, kzap, kzap.

The deadly sphere sent out lances of energy that melted narrow columns of rovlings before it.

Kzap, kzap, kzap, kzap. Boooom.

One of the beams cut through fifteen rovlings to detonate a specialized bombardier rovling at the end, destroying even more rovlings.

Yes! Take that you bastards!

Barrai took the opportunity to retreat under cover of the counterattack. She abandoned her empty launcher and ducked low in the cupola. Then she picked up the new launcher along with her backup force field pack, activated her stealth sphere, and fell back to another hardpoint deeper in the ship. The sounds of battle reverberated through the *Sharplight* all around her.

Kzap, kzap, kzap, kzap. Booom. Boooom.

She glanced at her Rovan shield interface and felt shock. Somehow, she had absorbed enough punishment to use up half its energy store. It seemed impossible that projectiles had drained that much energy. She wondered if a special model had hit her with a beam weapon.

Barrai left her second missile launcher live and ready to fire in a hallway, pointed the way the rovlings would come and set for their target signatures. It would fire its salvos without her.

Barrai readied her PAW, flipped off her stealth, and ran the rest of the way to the next laser emplacement. The emplacement sat at a big intersection of ship's corridors, above an armored island she had constructed using steel from the Rovan base.

She was deeper in the ship now, near the spinner. She had no grenades on her; the few left were set in boobytraps at key spots all around the ship. She expected each could get ten kills the way they were configured, but that was a drop in the bucket.

The tactical told her that the battle sphere had cleaned up the atrium and moved on. Rovlings were still flowing into the atrium, but the battle sphere had been programmed to keep on the move to help prevent the enemy from overwhelming it. Its energy production was lower than the

Vovokan counterparts; if it became energy-starved it
would be too easy to kill.

Rovlings stormed the corridor that Barrai had fled
through to get to her second position. The emplacement
above her opened up on them, slagging a dozen into the
floor. Barrai pointed her PAW down the corridor to the
right of that one and waited. Within the minute, rovlings
appeared at the far end.

Her weapon unleashed a torrent of small-caliber
rovling-killer rounds.

Ratatatatatat. Ratatatatatat.

The weapon's mild popping noise belied its
effectiveness on the rovlings. In Space Force slang, the
rovlings had gone all out for the A&F approach: Agile and
Fragile. The machines collapsed and spun across the floor,
collecting into heaps of debris.

Predictably, more rovlings emerged with no regard for
the devastation visited upon their vanguard. Barrai kept
firing.

Ratatatatatat. Ratatat! Splang! Zing!

A rovling with a larger armored body waddled
forward, unaffected by Barrai's rounds. Without missing a
beat, Barrai tried her breaker claw on it.

KA-BOOOM!

Barrai actually laughed out loud. Her instinct to try the
breaker claw had come out of nowhere, and worked! But
the charging rovlings did not abate.

Rovlings started to come out of holes blown in the
corridor walls and ceiling. Some fell through the rent deck,
but many others streamed on.

Snap. Crack. Pzang!

Rovling fire came in at her. She brought up her shield, dropped her stealth, reloaded her PAW, and resumed firing.

Ratatatatatat. Ratatatatatat.

The rovlings splattered all over the corridor, already piling up enough to obscure the end. Her weapon could kill them faster than they appeared, but even its immense clips drained in what seemed like no time.

Ratatatatatat. Ratatatatatat.

She was out of ammunition. She raked the corridor with its laser, killing dozens more before the energy cell gave up. She dropped the PAW. A rain of sparks came down upon her, signaling the end of the laser emplacement.

She dipped under her steel cover and regarded the four powered batons at her hips.

Am I really down to these again?

The tactical showed the battle raging all across the ship, but Barrai sensed that the rovlings might prevail again despite all her improvements. One of the battle spheres had died. The other two were finally pinned down and unable to withdraw. It was time to try one of her experimental strategies that could turn the tide in her favor.

Barrai bolted from cover.

Whap. Zing. Bam. Clink.

Despite the suddenness of her appearance, several rounds struck her shield. She darted into the nearest crash tube. The sliding door whisked shut. At her command, the tube filled with foam.

Let's shake this place up. Hard.

Barrai fed energy into the spinner. The *Sharplight* had taken widespread damage, but it still managed to deliver about thirty-five percent of its normal power to the gravity spinner. Barrai let a strong field spool up. During those few seconds, she disabled a dozen safety features in quick succession. Then she started to rotate the field.

At first, she slid against the foam this way and that. Then she started to slosh around more violently. The entire ship shuddered.

Die you bastards.

Forces pulled at her from ever-changing directions, often rapidly switching to opposite vectors to inflict maximum thrash damage. Barrai started to feel ill. A deep throb spread into her lungs. As the ship's energy reserves dropped, she decided she could take no more anyway. She halted the attack and told her tube to clear out and release her.

She checked the ship's status through her link. Though the ship had been rattled violently, its basic structure had survived the partial-energy spinner thrashing. The hull and most systems were not damaged, except where rovling sabotage had weakened them sufficiently.

Barrai examined what video feeds she had left as the foam drained.

Many rovlings had been damaged. The dog-sized octopeds had been smashed around, flying from floor to ceiling and to floor again, rolling around in tubes and crashing into structural supports, bulkheads, and each other. Some even lay dead. But most of the rovlings had weathered it, and the ship was not producing enough energy for another round of gravity disruption in the spinner-dampened zone of space near the Rovan battleship.

Barrai staggered out of the tube. Her arms shook and her legs trembled. The hallway looked bad. Panels had been ripped free down its length.

Rovlings charged her from both sides. The closest one limped, but moved well enough anyway… until Barrai smashed it to bits with a powered baton.

Bang. Whack. Zing! Smack.

The rovlings fired at her, but her personal shield held. She waded in with both weapons, crushing several more with satisfying swings. Barrai enjoyed it immensely, but she knew that she could not possibly kill enough with hand-to-hand weapons.

The nearest armory waited nearby. She charged forward, still swinging, to slog her way toward it. When her arms tired, she returned the batons to her belt and used laser pistols to make it the rest of the way.

When she arrived at the alcove entrance to the armory, her force field was down to ten percent. Barrai ducked inside to swap her packs. She activated her stealth sphere and dropped the spent pack.

When she lifted the next pack to swing over her shoulder and secure it, she realized something was wrong. The pack had a ragged hole in one side. Somehow, it had taken damage despite being close to or on her person the whole time. An ozone smell warned her that the pack had shorted.

Dammit. Maybe it got hit in the cupola before I picked it up? There goes my next phase.

Barrai had planned on wading back in and taking out a ton more rovlings. Now, she had to skip that step and go straight to guerilla warfare using her stealth pack. She hefted a laser rifle from the armory rack, grabbed extra energy clips for it, and ran out.

Dodging rovlings in the broken corridors under the protection of her cloaking sphere, she reviewed her strategy.

Focus on the special models. Take those out, and the others will suffer from lack of special support from combined arms.

The tactical showed that another battle sphere had died. There was only one left. Perhaps she could save it. She altered her route to take a position at one of its flanks.

Barrai took a sharp left turn and saw another group of rovlings ahead. Among them she saw a larger one with a bulging, rounded body. Its normal-sized companions gave it plenty of space.

Bombardier, she surmised. Barrai targeted it.

Hisssss. BOOOM!

The rovling exploded with enough force to rock the entire corridor. The bones of the *Sharplight* shuddered around her.

The surviving rovlings charged in several directions, trying to find the threat. Barrai cradled her rifle and waited. The weapon had the target sig of a special sensor-equipped rovling loaded at the highest priority. As soon as anything showed up that could reveal her, she would blow it away.

She took several more cautious steps toward her friendly machine. Her tactical had degraded, but it believed the ally machine to be within fifty meters of her position. She increased speed.

Thwack. Zing.

Projectiles started slinging by her. Something stung her back. She turned around. In an instant, her rifle identified a sensor support rovling and took it out. Then she whirled back and kept running.

The battle sphere had found the sheltered end of an open area to cover in. The hull of the ship was at its flank, reducing its defensive perimeter. Barrai caught a glimpse of it and informed it of her presence. Then she pointed her rifle out into the open zone and let it hit two or three specialized rovlings. It reported kills on a bombardier and two special models suspected to have heavy energy weapons.

Rovlings charged in from all directions, but they could not yet see her. Two more bombardiers became visible. Barrai hesitated. Should she be shooting these, or keep looking for the sensor-equipped ones?

Kzap, kzap, kzap, kzap. Boooom.

A wave of fire from the Terran battle sphere wiped them all out. Now the sphere would be out of juice for a time. She had to help it.

Barrai crouched against a battle-scarred wall, still cloaked, and waited. Another wave of rovlings massed ahead. Her laser rifle discharged several times, sniping off specialized rovlings until its pack was dead. She put in the next pack, but the weapon reported a malfunction. She saw that the end of the rifle had been damaged somehow.

Barrai cursed and pulled her batons again. She stepped forward to meet the oncoming wave of enemies, trying to stay out of the battle sphere's main field of fire.

The battle sphere came out of the alcove to join her.

Kzap, kzap, kzap.

It vaporized rovlings to either side, but stopped shooting quickly. It had expended its rings again and could not keep firing.

Rovlings charged them.

Barrai smashed two rovlings in two seconds and took another step forward.

Crackle… SNAP! Clang. Crunch.

The Terran battle sphere behind her fell to the deck and made a half-roll, then settled. Burn marks covered its blackened, pocked surface.

All the rovlings in the vicinity started to focus their fire on Barrai.

She scanned the area for the sensor rovlings that must be highlighting her position, but she could not spot them in time. Some of the enemies hit her with lasers. The cloaking device struggled to keep her hidden, but the energies involved were too high.

Barrai switched on her Rovan pack. Her weakened force field flickered under the barrage. She had to surrender now.

Damn these things! Damn them.

Barrai threw aside her stun batons and let herself be surrounded.

Thwack! Thwack! Snap!

Rounds struck her Veer suit. She felt a sharp pain in her right side. The force field had already failed. Barrai tried to process the repercussions of that, but a blast of energy struck her and snuffed out her consciousness.

Michael McCloskey

Chapter 12

Cilreth got up from her VR lounge on the Terran *Iridar* and stretched her legs. She had been studying materials provided by the scientists on Blackhab working on Vovokan and Rovan technology. A lot of other material related to the other races had been loaded into the ship's cache, but Cilreth did not touch it.

Quarus. Celaran. Rovan. I was happy just trying to learn about Vovokan computers.

Cilreth shook off the gloomy thoughts. No Terran would know everything about all the races. Caden and Cilreth had once been Celaran experts; now they were knowledgeable but far behind everything the Space Force and the Blackhab scientists had learned as a result of the Pact. More recently, Caden and Siobhan had been soaking up as much of the new material as they could. The PIT team could already do a lot more with the stealth spheres and lift rods than they used to be capable of; perhaps new miracles of technical integration awaited.

Cilreth believed she would still be valuable to the team as long as she updated her Vovokan knowledge and got in a basic review of the new aliens, the Rovans.

The PIT crew that had left from Blackhab had more to study than just the alien technologies; they had the unenviable task of trying to catch up on events the PIT team had experienced in their absence. Lee had provided some answers, but left many other questions unanswered.

Cilreth could see Telisa's hands in everything that had changed. The team members had better equipment than ever before, from advanced Celaran stealth to Rovan portable shields to Magnus's experimental anti-rovling weapons. The training scenarios were more oriented toward stealth and survival rather than straight-up combat capability. They still got lots of combat practice from the scenarios, but mostly from when they screwed up.

And it was almost time to practice with it all. The team's first VR scenarios of the voyage started in less than an hour. Cilreth was ambivalent; on one hand, she did not usually enjoy the violence of the scenarios they trained through, on the other, it would be a nice break from her studies.

Cilreth opened a locker built into the wall of her quarters and took out her OCP gear. The team was scheduled to do some pseudo-sim exercises after the full VR session to build up some muscle memory for maneuvering with the extra weight of the packs.

Orbs, Claws, and Packs. Interesting.

Cilreth reminded herself that the breaker claws would not typically destroy the average rovling. The light, agile creatures did not make use of energy storage rings. However, some specialized models of rovlings or other kinds of Rovan equipment might still explode from a claw attack.

Cilreth's door told her Siobhan had arrived. Cilreth told the door to let her guest in.

Siobhan wore her OCP over a Veer suit set to an olive-green hue. She smiled at Cilreth.

"Hi," Siobhan said. "You ready to frag-n-slag some of these Rovan creepy crawlies?"

"Rovlings, yes," Cilreth replied.

They walked together to the gym. On the way, Cilreth told the workout area to deploy for pseudo-VR. A video feed showed dark blue padding covering the walls and floor at their destination.

"I was thinking, Caden and I might have survived if we had had these force field backpacks with us on that mission."

Cilreth nodded. "I might have still been toast. I bet Imanol would still have died, too. I don't think the force field would work against being squished by gravity."

"Being squished? I resemble that comment," Imanol said, walking up to them.

"I guess since you don't remember the event, you're not too sore about it," Cilreth said.

Imanol shrugged.

"The poor guy probably didn't have a chance to feel any pain."

"The poor guy? It was *you*," Cilreth said.

"A copy. A great copy, I'm sure, but, not *this* bundle o' mass and energy," Imanol replied, tapping his thumb into his chest.

"We all have to die, eventually," Siobhan said. "Particular copies, I mean. I find it very reassuring to know that I'll be made again very soon."

Caden walked into the room.

"I'm with Imanol on this one," he said. "I value *my* life... *this* copy's life... independently of the idea that my pattern is stored somewhere in a Trilisk column ready to be built."

"Immortal but not immortal," Imanol said. "Thanks, Shiny," he sneered.

"It's not Shiny anymore," Caden pointed out.

Imanol made a face. "Let's just get started."

"Fine. What's first?" Caden asked.

"Lee gave me the latest training package from Telisa. She had special instructions just for us, should we be awakened," Cilreth said. "The first scenario is a rovling attack. We won't have any of the special weaponry Magnus designed."

"Ah. So the first one is one of those 'you-will-lose' lessons," Imanol said.

Should I tell them this is likely more about being smart, not deadly? I guess if they learn that themselves, maybe they'll learn it better.

"Probably," Cilreth said. "At least there's only one scheduled. Then we get to equip ourselves with anything from the new arsenal."

"Okay, let's get it over with," Caden said. He set his Rovan pack on the floor and sat cross-legged next to it. Cilreth followed suit and linked into the full sim.

Cilreth found herself inside a Rovan complex. The white corridors had a narrow ceiling with light panels. The walls sloped outwards to form a wide floor. She saw several evenly spaced bands of red wrapping the corridor, like lines on a game field.

The team moved forward, weapons ready, absorbing the feel of a Rovan environment.

Soon the rovlings came. Cilreth kept her cool, knowing it was a simulation… at first. The entire team covered well and used their arms to reasonable effect, but the alien machines just kept coming. It was unnerving. Cilreth fought off a wave of panic when her weapon emptied, then another as the first couple of rovlings engaged her in machete-to-leg-blade combat.

At the end of the first run, the entire team was overrun by blade rovlings. They gratefully came out of VR.

It felt very quiet in the gym.

"Fracksilvers," Siobhan breathed. "We were literally cut to pieces."

"It was virtual, so you can't say we were literally cut to pieces," Imanol said.

"Yes I can. We were literally cut to virtual pieces."

"Okay, well, lesson learned. Thank you Telisa," Cilreth said.

"We didn't need to go through that," Imanol said.

"She wanted to give us an appreciation for the new equipment, I'm sure," Caden said.

Imanol grimaced again.

"The new arsenal is available. Load out, and we start again in five," Cilreth said.

Cilreth went into the virtual armory and examined the new weapons available for the next round. Magnus had designed new shotguns, missile launchers, and ultra-small caliber submachine guns with long clips. Cilreth had always preferred pistols—stunners and lasers—but there were no new models of those. She took a submachine gun and two laser pistols with extra power packs. She stacked on the grenades, tripling her supply from two to six. She traded in her ordinary machete for an ultrasharp.

She saw that there were special Veer boots with short, wide blades deployable from the tips. She almost laughed, then thought about the combat again. Even with her training, Cilreth was not an expert in the martial arts, but she selected the boots anyway.

What the hell. Could be damn useful.

The team assembled in a vast Rovan bay. Super-wide corridors, big enough for multiple Rovans, led away in three directions. Once again the team deployed with the mission of finding a special computation room and retrieving the data stored there.

Within five minutes, they were set upon by rovlings. This time, they responded calmly with the new hardware. Cilreth used her weapon to shoot several of the first enemies to allow the others to wait and use their larger weapons later. Cilreth found the shotguns Imanol and Siobhan had taken to be devastating against clumped-up rovlings.

The scenario lasted much longer. They managed to find the target room, but ended up hopelessly pinned there until they had run out of ammunition and force field power. They tried to stealth themselves, but the corridor near the target room was narrow and already packed with rovlings. They rallied and tried to charge out with force fields, swords and batons, but the slog just tired them out and ran down their shields.

The end was the same, though they had tripled their kill count. They emerged to talk strategy incarnate. Imanol started them off.

"Come on, guys, use your heads," Imanol scolded. "With these rovlings it's all about crowd control. We don't need precision, we need area effect. The best thing we have are these multi-blast-cone grenades. One grenade, four to eight rovlings dead."

"We'll still lose if they just keep coming," Siobhan said. She sounded angry but Cilreth thought she detected a sliver of the same thing she felt: fear.

Fear of an enemy so numerous, that to fight them was nothing but a long, hard death.

"They may keep coming in all the scenarios," Cilreth told them. "We can work to increase combat efficiency, but we should also look into ways to avoid the confrontations that we're inevitably going to lose. So think up new approaches. We need to show some major improvement to make it through the harder missions."

"Like I said," Imanol drawled. "Use your heads. Caden. Why are you still using your sniper rifle?"

"I can carry several energy packs for the laser. And it works great for taking out the special designs, like the sensor ones and the exploding ones."

"Hey, that's worth doubling down on," Siobhan said. "What if two of us took sniper rifles, and we blew away all their sensor rovlings? Then all four of us could stay stealthed and take them out, however long it takes. Hit and run, or even just find a way to sneak through the rest."

"Okay, we have at least two things to try out," Cilreth said. "Let's load up on grenades first as Imanol suggests. Then we'll switch and try out the sniper rifle and cloaking approach. Ready?"

They went back in. And again. And again. They worked up to five times their original kill count. Their best strategy was to use stealth and mobility early on, then switch to the shields when they became trapped by overwhelming numbers of rovlings.

After about ten scenarios, everyone was ready to stand up and try out some pseudo-VR. They strapped their heavy Rovan packs onto their backs and donned headgear to feed their eyes and ears. Then they strapped on fake PAWs, pistols, and stun batons.

Cilreth chose a padded alcove and flipped her helmet down.

She saw a blank field. The silhouette of a PAW flashed before her. She pulled the PAW off her shoulder and held it ready.

She ran through a series of exercises that required her to maneuver in combat scenes piped through her helmet. The conveyor floor beneath her feet started to move. It could rotate in any direction to keep her within her alcove.

At first, she practiced running for cover and replying with her PAW.

Then the demands rose, having her use her baton in virtual combat. Cilreth started to breathe heavily, though her Veer suit kept her cool by drawing in air with every movement and using it to evaporate her sweat and carry the hot, moist air away.

Cilreth was really feeling the exertion as she worked through the last series of drills, which had her dodging and retreating in the face of a superior enemy. Her muscles began to fail under the heavy load. She tripped and fell, pried herself up, and kept going. Her legs felt like they were on fire by the time the simulation ended.

Cilreth pulled up her helmet and tossed it aside, uncaring. She stomped out of the alcove.

"My legs!" Siobhan lamented to Cilreth's right. Siobhan let her pack slip off and set it down, then staggered in a circle. Cilreth swallowed her own complaints. At least she had grown up in Earth gravity, unlike her tall and slender teammate.

"The packs are amazing. I mean who hasn't wanted a force field to protect them from bullets and lasers? But it's heavy, no doubt about it," Caden said. He panted, but sounded more enthusiastic by far than Cilreth felt.

Cilreth sat for a moment, luxuriating in collapse. She thought about Telisa. She knew their leader had always hated having to sometimes fight the aliens they discovered.

She must be so disappointed to have to fight the Rovans. She always said our team is supposed to just be explorers.

Cilreth decided to get a shower. When she came to her feet, she felt a sudden snap in the back of her calf muscle.

"Argh!"

"What?" Siobhan asked.

"The pack was worse than I thought. My calf just ripped!"

"I'd offer to carry you to the med bay, but then we'd have two injured people," Siobhan said.

"I can help you," Caden offered.

"Thanks you guys. It's okay. Just a strain. I'll limp over there and get the muscle weaver to fix it up."

Cilreth limped off toward the bay. It was slow going, but the Terran *Iridar* was not a huge ship. She made it to the medical center in a few minutes.

She gratefully found a seat on one of the low scanner beds. A spindly robot came to life beside the bed.

"Please recline," it said. The machine did not need to ask her about the injury, since it could ask her Veer suit which had already been tracking the tissue damage.

"Please release the suit to me for treatment," the machine said.

Cilreth told her Veer suit to cooperate fully.

A drug dispensary connected to her suit and let it add some medicine to her circulatory system. Then her leggings were removed smoothly. A warm robot arm raised her injured leg and held it for the muscle weaver to work on.

Her status report became available as it worked. Cilreth idly looked through it as she waited.

Suddenly a pane in the report caught her attention. A graph had changed dramatically; a line rose to a red peak, then dropped back into the green in a discontinuity.

"By the tentacle!"

My twitch damage is gone! The Trilisk column must have removed it for me.

Cilreth wanted to tell someone. That person would have been Telisa. She recalled that being on the PIT team was kind of lonely. It was rare for a Terran of her generation to not spend their days on the network.

What would she say? Announce that the whole team should start using it?

Cilreth walked back to her quarters with her head spinning. She had thought about the tradeoff she was making to be a twitch user so many times, it had become part of her psyche: she was burning brighter, but at a cost to her life.

Many kinds of genetic treatments were known to Terran medicine, but canceling out the long term effects of the drug was not one of them. The drug changed Terran cells to produce new receptor structures that significantly changed the way the cells functioned. Attempts to use nanobots to remove the structures had always resulted in terrible consequences.

I suppose I shouldn't be surprised. It makes sense... the Trilisks can do anything, and why create a body with a flaw? It can just be edited out.

Cilreth went into her quarters, hit her bed, and fell asleep.

***

Cilreth forced herself to look at some basics of Rovan cybernetics they had learned on Blackhab. It was a lesson in what could exist in a bubble devoid of lies and ill intent. Security had always been at odds with convenience. Rovan systems might be naive, simple-minded even, but when input went unchecked, processes ran without worry for authorizations, and entire subsystems did not have to be constantly audited for subversion of purpose, it made for a fast, clean environment indeed.

A Vovokan computer was as byzantine as their subterranean cities by comparison.

Maybe learning two technologies wouldn't be so bad after all.

After a couple of hours, Cilreth had returned to her previous cynicism. Alien systems were just that—alien— and while she recognized some of the same basic data structures that Terrans, Vovokans, and Celarans used, after that it always got weird. She swore learning computer science had not been so hard when she was young—or was it just that she thought like a Terran?

She decided to try out her new calf muscle by walking out to get lunch. As she strode out of her quarters, she monitored her injured leg closely. Was that a touch of stiffness, or just her imagination?

She wandered into the mess hall. Imanol was there, eating a tangled pile of protein and carb noodles. Cilreth heated up a calzone and joined him.

"Hey. About our training earlier? Maybe back off the bitterness just one notch, before everyone forgets that they missed you," Cilreth said.

"Whatever you say, Twitch Queen," Imanol said glumly.

"You should also take it easy on me. We're the old guard. We should stick together," Cilreth argued.

Imanol leaned against the back of his chair. His face softened somewhat.

"I hear you. We've been out of the game the longest, and we're not kids. We won't bounce back as fast."

"Well, about the bouncing back… my twitch damage is gone."

"Ah, the new and improved Cilreth, eh? Congratulations. A young woman now, are we?"

Cilreth laughed.

"The struggle is along a new axis, now," she said.

"How so?"

"So much has happened! I can't handle this new tech. I invested a huge amount of effort learning about Vovokan systems. I tried to start in with the Rovan stuff, but… I'm balking. And I'm sure if Marcant is still alive, he's learned a ton about the Vovokan stuff while I was gone."

"While you were dead," Imanol corrected calmly. "While *we* were dead… we passed the Alexander time of these subjects."

"What's the Alexander time?"

"Something Maxsym told me about. There was a time, if you go back far enough, when one person could be educated with the total of all Terran knowledge. That passed. Then as each new branch of science came into being, there was a time in its infancy when one person could learn everything that was known about it. For a while, you were one of those people. You knew all that was known by Terrans about Vovokan stuff. Now, it's being studied by hundreds of people, and more all the time, and we know too much for any one person to get it all."

"Yes. With focus and commitment, I could still know everything there is to know about Vovokan toothbrushes. Or sand toilets. Anything broader than that and my brain won't hold it, even with my link's assistance."

"Telisa values you highly," Imanol said. "Marcant is a snotheaded incomalcon. Even if you only understand Terran and Vovokan computers, that's one and a half more technologies than I know about."

Cilreth smiled. Imanol had just called someone else a malcontent?

Marcant may be a malcontent, but he's no incompetent.

"Well, you fragged twice as many rovlings in the simulations today than I did. So you're still useful, too. I guess they won't throw us in an airlock just yet."

Imanol nodded.

"Not just yet."

Chapter 13

Arakaki opened her eyes. She pulled in a deep breath, then rose up from a cold surface.

"Yat?" she whispered.

There was no answer. She shivered in the cool air of a lab. Her torso and hips were covered only in her translucent undersheers.

Arakaki slid off the platform carefully, testing her strength. She felt herself for wounds.

Suddenly she thought of the rovlings. Were they here? Hiding nearby?

She scanned the lab. A shelf across the room had her Veer suit sitting on it. She walked over to get it and found her PAW, a knife, and a stun baton.

I have to find Yat. Maybe they took him, too.

Arakaki pulled her Veer suit on quickly, keeping watch for any movement. Then she took her weapons and searched the lab area for any signs of Yat. She found only more platforms, two of them Rovan-sized, more tanks, and bins of mysterious tools of all shapes. She imagined the lab might be a medical bay, but she could not tell anything for sure.

She found a three-meter wide door and approached it. The door opened. Arakaki walked out into a clean hallway with the Rovan-style trapezoidal shape: A narrow ceiling above outward-sloping walls that joined a wide floor.

Arakaki contemplated her memory of arrival. She selected the direction the rovlings had dragged her from, seeking to retrace her route back to Yat. She felt vulnerable without her attendants. She had nothing to scout ahead and no live feed of her six o'clock.

Amazing how attached I've become to those Vovokan robots.

The corridor came to another wide door instead of the intersection Arakaki had expected.

Dammit! I must have missed a turn in the fight. How could I be so stupid?

She thought about turning back, but decided that Yat might be in the room ahead, perhaps even being examined or tortured. She stepped forward and the door opened wide to let her in.

The large room before her had rows of display anchors along its circular wall. There was enough space for ten or fifteen Terrans to have worked inside, but Arakaki supposed it might have accommodated only four or five Rovans. She saw feeds from each anchor.

On one, a Rovan ship sat next to a dead hulk. On another, she saw the *Sharplight*. She quickly took several steps forward to watch it more closely.

What? They're here! Looking for us!

A bank of virtual controls sat below the video feed.

This makes no sense. How can my link receive a Rovan feed? How could I have access to their controls? They must have figured out our links and integrated mine... why would they do that?

As she watched, the *Sharplight* started to fire. It took a moment for Arakaki to realize it was firing point defense weapons, not the main batteries. The feed flickered as the ship engaged electromagnetic defenses to confuse the incoming missiles. Some vaporized as they approached. Other missiles hit home but did not explode.

They're fighting for their lives. How can I help?

She looked over the controls. Could she affect the battle? Would she be able to work them without making things worse?

Surely an idiot at the controls could only make it worse for the Rovan side...

Movement on another screen caught her eye.

It was Magnus, pacing a cell like the one Yat and her had shared. Arakaki stepped aside to take a quick look and see if he was all right. Magnus seemed bored but otherwise not in distress.

She looked at the next anchor point to her right. It was a feed of Yat.

"Yat! Yat, can you hear me?"

Arakaki stepped in front of the feed. She watched as the door opened to Yat's cell. Rovlings poured in. She watched in horror as they charged at Yat.

"What the hell?" Arakaki looked for virtual controls nearby, but the feed had none.

The rovlings overpowered Yat and wrestled him down. He yelled and fought, then was still.

Arakaki balled her fists and stood aghast at the screen.

"Frag you bastards!"

The rovlings broke away, except for couple of them that walked over Yat's prone form as if waiting for more resistance. The other rovlings left through the door while the two near Yat remained.

The door stayed open.

Yat!

Arakaki turned to bolt out of the room. She had to find the prison cell.

She ran from the room and back down the corridor. She arrived back at the lab and followed the corridor the other direction, still running.

She came to an intersection. She turned and stared back toward the lab to orient herself and compare to memory. She decided to take the passage right and keep going.

When she took another turn and saw an open low door on a long, vertical wall, she redoubled her haste.

"Yat! Yat can you hear me?" the called both aloud and through her link.

The door was low, rovling-height, so she charged toward it at full speed, then slid through the cell door on her side, ready to do battle.

Yat was not inside. Instead, a huge Rovan sat on the base of its shell in the center of the room. It had a shiny blue shell and a shockingly orange head.

A Rovan!

She aimed her PAW at the alien's head.

"What have you done with Yat?" she snarled.

"Two Terrans kept here -investigation needed- no Terrans kept here. Terran arrives to attack Rovan -Terran stopped- situation delta?"

"Stop messing with us. We're not your enemy. We're trying to figure out what happened to all of you! We only want to be your friends, but your rovlings keep mistaking us for enemies."

"Terran arrives to find Rovan -Rovan found- situation delta?"

"Situation delta? Uhm. Terran wants her friend. Then we want to be treated as your friends."

A real, biological rovling scuttled up to the Rovan. Arakaki heard a startling sound like a rattlesnake's warning. She stared at the side of the Rovan. A taught, cylindrical structure vibrated at the center of the Rovan's side port. The rovling stepped into the port and settled itself atop the appendage, which slipped into the rovling's ventral organ.

Arakaki's face grimaced in dismay.

Ugh! These things are more grotesque than I thought.

She noted that the Rovan had not moved an inch since she found it. Despite its monstrous legs, the thing struck her as sessile. She watched two more natural rovlings walk around it searchingly.

The rovlings do all the work. The Rovan just… sits there and thinks?

She returned her gaze to the formidable head. The two foremost eyes on the top stared down at her like the wide-set orbs of a huge praying mantis.

How did this thing get in here, anyway? And why would it be here… I saw Yat on the screen and ran here...

"Is this even real?" Arakaki said. She decided to try and phrase it more as she had been receiving it from the alien. "Terran captured, Rovan replaces link, Terran sees the deception."

"Terran captured -Rovan studies- situation delta?"

She saw her mistake immediately. It did not understand her last part. The Rovans lack of security pointed to it: they did not deceive each other. But had they learned that aliens could lie? Perhaps their enemies had taught them that lesson.

"Terran captured, Rovan replaces link... Terran knows this is virtual."

"Rovan ready to defend -Terran invades- Rovan studies alien."

"I can tell you a lot about myself if you do the same," Arakaki said. "My name is Arakaki. I'm an explorer. Who are you? Are you alone here? We found empty Rovan worlds."

"Rovans wanted mind -created this mind- Rovans gone."

Arakaki pondered that one.

Did it just say it's an AI?

"Please let me go," Arakaki urged.

"Arakaki confined -Rovan grants request- Arakaki free. Arakaki free -mutation?"

Arakaki struggled to interpret the seeming question.

That's the first time it didn't use three parts. The second part is a change… so maybe it wants to know what my change would be.

"Arakaki released. We go search for more Rovans together. We find them and cooperate, be friends, learn from each other."

"Rovan mind studying Arakaki -knowledge gained- situation upgrade. This Rovan starship in position -time passes- This Rovan starship in position."

It's not going anywhere. But it did not rule out becoming my friend.

Arakaki sighed. She was not getting anywhere quickly, but interaction could only improve her plight—she hoped.

"Fine. Study me. What will you study next?"

"Arakaki knows of me -memory erased- Arakaki returns to ignorance."

"What—" she said, then plunged into darkness.

Chapter 14

Marcant saw the suspected rovling carrier as a dot of off-white in the void. So far from a star, it would have been utterly invisible without the aid of his space suit sensors.

"Leave an attendant out here," Telisa ordered. "We need a good relay to make sure we can talk with Adair, as well as a lookout in case surviving rovlings come back."

"Will do," Maxsym said.

Telisa turned in the shuttle seat toward Marcant.

"Okay, this feels familiar. Moving equipment in and out of shuttles," she said to him.

Marcant looked at the oblong missile next to him. The Vovokan weapon was lighter than one would expect, but it still outweighed any of the Terrans.

He sealed his helmet onto the space suit he wore over his Momma Veer. It reported all systems green. Maxsym and Telisa were similarly prepared.

Marcant patted the Vovokan weapon next to him like a pet.

Don't let us down, Mr. Missile.

"Stealth," Telisa ordered. They blinked out to be replaced by their ghostly counterparts.

"Let's hit it," Telisa said.

The shuttle cargo area opened to the cold vacuum of interstellar space. Marcant guided his Vovokan charge out by a tether, then released it to float slowly away.

"Adair, how's it going?" Telisa asked as she exited the ghostly green shuttle silhouette.

"No signs that the rovlings might be leaving any time soon."

"Good. We'll be using the missile soon. Make yourself scarce."

"Oh, I'm on it."

"Marcant, you untethered the missile, right? It's hard for me to see from your sensor ghost."

"Yes, it's released."

The missile moved smoothly away at an ever-increasing pace. The plan was for it to take up a position where it could get a clear run at the dead hulk where the rovlings worked.

Telisa waved them on. They left the cloaked shuttle. The external attendant tagged along with them as they used their suits to accelerate gently toward the target.

The stars moved across his faceplate. For some reason, they inspired even more awe in Marcant than usual, because he was aware of his position out between stars, in a suit instead of a starship, just floating with mind-boggling distances between himself and every place he had ever known.

They approached the tiny Rovan craft.

"You're on, Marcant. Open this thing, please," Telisa said.

Marcant saw from the tactical that they had closed to within fifty meters of the transport. It was so dark, he could barely see it at all.

"Do we need to illuminate it?" Telisa asked. "We probably can; these lights are so weak I don't think the battleship could pick them up. We could place this thing between us and the battleship and decloak."

"I doubt it. Our scans show this door at the end; I'll try and open that and hope it's a carrying bay."

Marcant started running their Rovan hacking programs. Their dirt simple ones failed. Marcant had half-expected that. He led the others over toward the door he wanted to open while the suite kept working on the door.

Telisa and Maxsym were patient. Marcant watched two more programs fail. He told one of is attendants to leave his cloaking field and scan the door. Some new structures were detected and displayed in an information pane of his PV.

"I see a redundant controller," he told his teammates. "I think it's not working so far because I need to coordinate with both of them at once. I'm starting over again."

Marcant remained calm and tried again, this time communicating with both of the suspected Rovan controllers.

As he waited again, Marcant told himself it would work just because these were Rovan systems. Hacking a Terran door like this might not take long, but that was because he knew all about Terran systems. Getting a new type of Vovokan door to open might take… forever.

Come on, Rovan door. You can trust me. I'm honest, just like you guys must have been.

The door opened. The illumination from inside seemed bright at first, like a white-hot sun. Then Marcant's suit filters and eyes adjusted. It was actually a very dim light by normal Terran standards. Marcant saw a long, empty chamber. There were dozens of niches in the wall which he assumed were resting places for closely-packed rovlings.

Telisa went in first. Marcant and Maxsym followed her. Marcant's attendant rejoined him but the other one remained stationed outside. Their stealthed shuttle had approached the Rovan vessel to within a quarter of a kilometer, ready to whisk them away if they encountered trouble.

"Close," Telisa said. Marcant asked the door to close as he looked for a place to secure himself.

"Should we uncloak?" Marcant asked.

"I don't see any sensors in here… it is a risk, but I want to save as much of our juice as we can, so let's try."

Telisa became visible. Maxsym and Marcant did the same a few seconds later.

"It occurs to me that this rovling carrier might accelerate at rates lethal to us," Marcant said.

"It might be a rough ride, but the rovlings aren't *that* durable," Maxsym said.

"Adair has seen these ships move about," Telisa said. "We might expect short bursts of more than 1g, but he thinks we can weather it."

He thinks...

"Adair. We're in. Proceed with the strike."

"Copy. You have thirty seconds."

Marcant took a deep breath. He accessed the attendant's feed from outside and waited for the flash of energy that would announce the rovling's demise.

"Wait. There's something coming out toward you," Adair said. Marcant brought up the tactical pane in his mind. It showed something coming right for the carrier.

"Is it a missile?!" Marcant asked. "Should I turn on my force pack?"

"No," Telisa said. "It's too slow. Probably rovlings."

Sweet purple paste from Gorgantor, the timing.

"Then what will we do?" Maxsym asked.

"We will stay calm and not panic," Telisa said firmly. "There are probably only a few coming back and this bay could hold at least twenty. Remember, we can always cloak and if all else fails... we can kill a few rovlings."

Marcant felt reassured by her words. It all made sense. If the Rovan craft reported them, they could always flee back to the shuttle.

The light of an explosion blossomed on the attendant feed. The light from the explosion lit up their guest: a single rovling. It landed upon the skin of the ship and clambered toward the same door they had entered.

"Fifty-fifty chance it will stay at the front or move to the back. Be on your toes in case it wants to take a seat in the rear," Telisa said. She gave the signal to cloak. Everyone winked out of sight.

The outer door opened. The rovling walked in like a huge insect. For some reason, Marcant felt afraid of it.

Just one rovling... we could kill it ten times over in a second.

It seemed to stare down into the empty bay for a second, then it rotated until its body fit the nearest indentation in the wall. It tucked up its legs and snuggled into the depression, then sat still.

No one made any comment for a minute. Marcant supposed they were just conserving power and being extra cautious. Then he felt the pull of acceleration. The tactical showed that the vessel was underway to the battleship.

"So that's their response," Maxsym said thoughtfully. "They're recalling this ship."

"Actually, they're both recalling the carrier and sending a squadron out to investigate," Adair informed them.

"Go silent and proceed to location one," Telisa instructed. "If our shuttle gets taken out, we'll send a directional signal to each preplanned location in order when we come back out with our team."

"Got it. Good luck," Adair said and dropped its connection.

Marcant stared at far hatch and suppressed a feeling of claustrophobia.

If Adair were here, it would remind me that I shouldn't worry about what will happen if the doors don't open. I should worry about what happens when they do *open.*

Marcant shuffled nervously.

"Be still," Telisa said. "Don't waste your cloaking sphere's power."

Yes. I am just a space barnacle. Sessile, harmless.

Marcant just breathed and watched the tactical. The acceleration was mild, then the small ship's spinner kicked in. He could see the journey would not take long.

He stared at the inside of the bay and wondered at the idea of being inside an alien ship. Who were the Rovans? What were the rovlings to them? Helpful robots? Stormtroopers? Beloved pets? All of that and more?

"We've stopped."

Anxiety grabbed Marcant and thrashed him back and forth.

"This is bad. That ship can vaporize us at any moment," Marcant said.

"Calm… maybe they don't lower the screens for just one ship," Telisa said.

"Or perhaps at least not when there are hostiles around," Maxsym suggested.

Or perhaps not when there are hostiles aboard…

They waited for another tense minute. Marcant's sudden unease subsided somewhat.

"If they do let us through at some point, should we abandon this crate before it goes into a bay? How will we get out if the door opens and a bunch of rovlings march right in?" Marcant asked.

"If we don't, we might be trapped outside the hull," Telisa said.

"We could have Marcant open a side door just as we slip into the battleship," Maxsym said reasonably.

"Yes, if you can open this door on our other side?" Telisa asked.

"I think so," Marcant said. He prepared the program that had worked on the far door for one of the doors on the other end, away from the rovling.

He completed the task and waited. The minutes dragged on. He had never anticipated being stuck outside the shields, just waiting. Apparently one transport vessel with a lone rovling was extremely low-priority when it came to lowering the shields.

They waited.

After half an hour, Telisa's green ghost stirred.

"This is draining too much of our stealth time. I'm going to kill it."

"You can't!" Marcant objected. "We're stationed just outside the battleship's shields. If they know something's wrong in here, they could fire on us."

"We can't save the others if we don't have most of our stealth time left," Telisa asserted.

Marcant watched her ghostly green outline through their orb connection. She raised a pistol and pointed it at the rovling.

Oh, this could be so bad…

"Stop! Something's happening," Maxsym said.

"Another ship is coming, this could be it," Telisa said. Her ghost put away the weapon and sat back.

Good! Oh. Unless the other ship is coming to investigate us.

Marcant watched the new red dot move across the tactical toward them. An information pane opened. It was a small Rovan ship the size of a Terran destroyer.

"It's on intercept with us," Maxsym said nervously.

"Relax guys. It's just going to come through the shields with this ship. Maybe they always wait in formation, or go through synchronously to minimize the shield down time."

"Let's hope that we don't have to wait for too many more ships to arrive before—" Maxsym started. He halted when the tactical highlighted new information.

The shields dropped. Marcant felt acceleration.

It worked!

Marcant let himself feel relief for a moment, then transitioned into anxiety about what would happen when they actually arrived.

"What about our shuttle?" asked Maxsym.

"It's coming in with us into the shields, but staying outside the hull. We can escape the ship from any lock and it can pick us up."

But then we'll be stuck inside the shields. Maybe Barrai could do the trick we did with the Rovan stations, and weaken the shields just long enough for us to burst out.

The Rovan ship they rode accelerated gently. It moved toward one of four kilometer-long fuselages that comprised the Rovan battleship. Marcant saw a large hangar door open to receive them. The size of the battleship hit home again: the cylinder they approached had a diameter of over a hundred meters, and it was only one of the four main sections of the ship. He saw that the four sections were joined to a thinner "spine" that extended even longer than a kilometer.

"Here we go," Telisa said. "Marcant, let's exit out this door instead, so we don't cross paths with the rovling."

The transport slipped inside the battleship. Marcant told the side door to open.

Life just a simulation, he told himself. *You should take a data page from Siobhan's cache and enjoy it more.*

Michael McCloskey

Chapter 15

Arakaki opened her eyes. She drew in a long breath.
"Hello?" she called softly.

No one responded.

Her back felt cold. She immediately wrapped her arms around herself and became aware that she had almost nothing on. It felt terrible to be in her undersheers, without her Veer suit.

Damn rovlings. What have they done to me?

Arakaki rose. She was on a flat platform. She recalled this was the lab where the rovlings had dragged her.

They took my Veer suit off to… what?

She examined herself for marks. Nothing seemed out of place. She did not even have bruises, as her Veer suit had protected her… until they removed it.

How did Rovans hack the suit? It would only have opened to save my life, or if they hacked it.

Arakaki stood up from the platform. Suddenly she saw her Veer suit and her PAW on a shelf over a stack of white-cased machines. She pounced on the suit, pulling it down and stepping into it as fast as she could. She grabbed the PAW and found a laser pistol and a powered baton next to it. She took everything.

What am I doing here? What's my mission?

She briefly examined the machines around her, but could not guess their function. Most were encased in smooth white material. A few had flat readout panes on the front, a few more had openings of various shapes and sizes. They all had cables and pipes running into and out of them, connecting into the floor or into each other.

Nothing in her environment cleared up her questions. She closed her eyes and remained calm.

I'm on a Rovan ship... an invader... I'm an explorer... or a soldier. What have they done to me to make me forget?

Suddenly Arakaki heard a shuffle. She slowly turned her head and looked down a walkway between the machines. At first she saw nothing, then... a Terran boot extended from behind a machine on the floor.

She turned her PAW and advanced. The boot was Veer, just like her own suit's footgear.

Must be a friend, right? Any Terran is a friend in a place like this...

Arakaki took the last few steps rapidly, standing before the niche to see who was there. A Terran sat in the spot with his back against the wall. When he saw Arakaki, he brought his head stiffly back and set it against the wall, as if resigning himself to death.

"Who are you?" she demanded.

"Garrison... Magnus Garrison," he said weakly.

"Arakaki. Are you Space Force?"

"Yes. I'm a shuttle and sublight propulsion specialist, UNSF *Galahad*."

Arakaki dropped the barrel of her weapon and knelt before him.

"Well, how did you end up here?"

"I... I don't remember," he said. His face pinched in concern. "How can I not remember?"

"The Rovans have been screwing with you," Arakaki said. Even as she said it, she wondered what they had done to her in the lab. Was she missing time, too?

"This is a… Rovan battleship, isn't it?" he asked. "What are we doing here?"

"Right now, we're just trying to get the hell out."

Magnus nodded. His face twisted in pain.

"You're injured."

"I don't know. My ribs… the pain is bad."

She accessed his Veer suit and got his health status. It showed cracked ribs and torn muscles, which had caused mild internal bleeding that had been halted by the suit's tiny medkit.

"I don't know how to get out of here. You rest here, I'll see what I can find."

"My link map has some parts of the ship on it," Magnus said. He shared his map with her. Arakaki threw the data onto a shared tactical.

"So we know which way you came from. Maybe that's the easiest way out," Arakaki said.

"Maybe."

"I'm going to scout it. If the way is clear to that lock, we might be able to arrange an extraction."

Magnus nodded.

"Do you have a weapon?"

"Just a knife."

Arakaki handed him her laser pistol.

"I'll be back."

"You're… giving me your pistol? That's a big risk."

"I'm not leaving you here defenseless," she said. "You're in no shape to use a knife." She winked, putting up a bit of bravado to raise his spirits.

"Thank you."

According to the link map, just around the turn was a Rovan corridor with twelve connecting rovling pipes. That would likely be the most dangerous section. She padded to the corner, wondering how well rovlings could hear.

Arakaki listened. She did not catch any sounds of rovling movement. She leaned over to take a peek. Nothing.

No point in trying to sneak through there… either they come out or not. So just minimize your exposure time.

Arakaki turned the corner and ran for it. Her heart pumped hard as she flew by each set of tubes. At the end of the corridor, she took one look back to see if anything had stirred. She did not see any rovlings, so she pressed herself next to the wall by a door.

Though she still had not recalled any details of what her purpose was on this alien ship, she found that she had tools to navigate it. Arakaki activated a software suite on her link that could open the Rovan doors. Though the door and her link were not designed to be compatible, the software knew how to fool the door.

The software raised a challenge: 'Provide justification for door breach'.

Arakaki cursed. Justification? What bureaucrat had written this?

"I'm trying to save a life and escape from a hostile ship."

The link showed an equipment room beyond. There were no annotations as to the purpose of the machines there. When the door opened, Arakaki slipped inside with her PAW ready. More alien machines dominated the room on each side. She padded through quickly, just trying to make it to the far side. There, she saw only a short corridor, this time with vertical side walls instead of the sloped walls that accommodated the Rovans and their rovlings' pipes.

The map showed the lock ahead and on the left. Arakaki stopped to listen again. Nothing. She told her link to open the last door. It rose, revealing a spacious Rovan space prep room. The airlock was visible on the far side.

Made it!

Arakaki moved forward carefully, though she saw no enemies. She looked over the Rovan bins, mounted at about waist level on the walls. The floor was slightly sloped down to a drain at the center. She assumed that was for a decontamination procedure.

Something in the corner looked out of place. Arakaki stepped forward with her PAW trained on the nook. Instead of a Rovan deck, the floor looked folded up. Arakaki took another step forward.

It was a Terran space suit. Arakaki queried its status; it reported itself operational, with five hours of air and power.

Maybe we can get out of here… if they haven't come back and found me gone.

Telisa thought about the suit. It was logically Magnus's or another Space Force person. Perhaps the suit knew about their pickup.

She got a code from the space suit and sent a transmission out. She immediately received a reply.

There's an unmanned shuttle out there! This must be how he arrived… maybe how both of us arrived.

Arakaki searched the rest of the lock from top to bottom. There were two large bins, but they held only a confusing array of Rovan equipment.

She sighed.

No second space suit. Nothing is ever easy.

Arakaki returned to Magnus as fast as she could. When she got back to the room where she had started, she saw that Magnus had not moved.

"There's one space suit in the lock and a Terran shuttle outside," Arakaki said. "Take the suit. Go check the shuttle. If there's a suit for me, great. Otherwise, just get the hell back to your ship if you can."

"You'll give the suit to me?"

"Yes. It's probably your suit anyway. That might be the *Galahad*'s shuttle out there," Arakaki told him.

"Why didn't you take the suit and go?" Magnus asked, incredulous.

How could he even ask that? We're fellow soldiers… I think.

"You're welcome," Arakaki said. "Now stand up."

Arakaki extended an arm to haul Magnus up. He started to stand, then fell back onto a low machine beside his hiding spot. Arakaki slid forward and put her arm under his, behind his back. She tried to brace herself to lift again.

"Thank you," he whispered, then kissed her.

Part of Arakaki wanted to tell him to get in the suit and escape, but a wave of emotion overcame her. Her head spun. She found herself leaning into the kiss.

She gently broke free.

"Don't we need to… escape…?"

Arakaki felt an intense attraction to the stranger she could not explain. Was this normal? Suddenly she felt unanchored to the entire situation, as if transitioning scenes in a dream.

"We're safe," Magnus said. "The Rovans are gone."

The words were so welcome, so pleasant, that Arakaki immediately believed them.

Magnus held her face in his calloused hands, then grabbed the collar of her Veer suit, pulling. She told her suit to open. The fastener unlocked, allowing him to pull the armored material apart.

I just got into this suit... I guess now I'm getting back out of it.

Michael McCloskey

Chapter 16

Telisa leaped from the transport door first. Her superhuman legs launched her swiftly away from the lip of the door to a ridged platform in the Rovan bay. An attendant feed told her that Marcant did the same a second later as the carrier vessel taxied in. Maxsym hesitated only a moment, then launched himself after Marcant. The other two landed intact, though less gracefully, alongside the walkway Telisa had targeted.

Once Telisa saw them ready, she led the way toward a hatch. She held up a hand to signal that they would wait. A huge white gate slowly rose to close off the bay. Telisa suddenly realized it was only an assumption that the bay would be pressurized at all; obviously the rovlings did not need the atmosphere, so perhaps the bay would remain empty?

The same thought might have occurred to Marcant and Maxsym. Their green sensor ghosts watched the gate carefully.

Once the bay had been sealed, Telisa waited. Her attendants and her Veer suit did not notice any pressure changes to report.

Hrm. Maybe this ship was never designed for Rovans. Or maybe just this section.

Telisa turned back to the hatch. There was no window. She examined the door, but there were no symbols or writing anywhere. That did not surprise her: in Terran spacecraft, all the warnings and directions would be piped through a link. She was aware of practices in antiquity where warnings had been placed in writing in strategic places, but of course, that failed to keep people safe in many scenarios. The Rovans, being so advanced, had likely left such days far behind as well.

Telisa pointed at the door and stepped aside. Marcant's ghost nodded and he stepped closer to the door.

As always, opening the door took just long enough to worry Telisa that something had gone wrong. When it finally opened, they slipped inside an airlock and the door shut behind them.

Telisa examined the hatches and the white interior.

Doesn't feel like a Rovan door, but it's big for a rovling one. It's probably sized to allow them to bring in cargo from the bay.

They cycled through the lock and emerged into a typical Rovan hallway with white sloped walls and red bands. The narrow ceiling provided light that shined down through hexagonal louvers. Gravity from the ship's spinner held them against a floor placed perpendicular to the spine of the ship, so the deck would be a circular slice of the long cylindrical section which now towered a half kilometer above and below them. That probably put the bow of the starship far above their heads, with the aft far below their feet.

"What now?" Maxsym asked.

"We stash our space suits. Explore. Minimize communication, though if you have a good idea about where to go, I'd like to hear it," Telisa said.

Telisa decided she wanted to stick to the corridors first, move rapidly, and get a feel for the layout of the deck. Their straight corridor soon met another with a gentle curve that probably matched the shape of the cylinder around them. Two rovlings moved along the corridor but soon dodged into rovling tubes.

Telisa led them full circle around the deck. It was a long walk, even at a hurried pace. Over a hundred rovling tubes emptied into the passage. Dozens of artificial rovlings moved about on unknown tasks, unaware of the PIT team. Telisa noted eighteen doors.

She pondered the best way to explore such a huge ship.

So the rooms are fairly large. I hope the entire deck is devoted to a particular purpose. That way, we could check one or two chambers and move on to another deck if it doesn't seem like someplace the Rovans would keep prisoners.

She checked her stealth orb. Hiding on the carrier vessel had been kind to their energy stores; she was reading over ninety percent charge. Still, to search a ship this size… they would have to make some good decisions to find the others before time ran out.

When they came back to the starting spot, Telisa pointed at a door facing toward the outside of the ship section. Marcant got it open very quickly.

The room was long. Telisa saw a curve to it that suggested it ran a significant part of the cylindrical fuselage they were in. Three elevated rovling-sized walkways led over an array of open-topped bins. Each bin was mobile, set on metal wheels, but none of them stirred.

Telisa peered into one. The bin had a confusing array of components within. Some looked distinctly metallic, but others could have been plastic, ceramic, or pure carbon. A distinct ovoid shell caught her attention.

That's a rovling top. These might be all the parts it takes to make a rovling. Or to make a particular repair.

She looked across that Marcant and Maxsym. They had pulled bins of their own and examined the contents.

"Stash the spacesuits here," she ordered. "We can get to the shuttle without them, if we have to."

As long as our Veer suits don't have huge gaping holes in them by that time.

Telisa removed the exterior suit, stuffed it into the bin, and pushed the bin back into place under the counter. Marcant and Maxsym copied her actions. It felt better to be back in nothing but 'Momma Veer and undersheers' or MVUs as the Space Force personnel liked to put it.

They resumed walking. After twenty meters, she spotted a rovling working on a flat table. One of the bins lay slightly below it, hanging from the edge of the work platform. As they came nearer, she saw that it worked to assemble a new rovling.

Rovlings can put together other rovlings. Hardly seems surprising, though it doesn't seem like the most efficient way to do it... shouldn't there just be an automated factory?

The rovlings were doubtless very versatile. It reminded Telisa a bit of the Celaran tools. Perhaps the Rovans shared that sensibility with the Celarans: was every task set up to be done by a rovling with fewer specialized machines? Was her critique just a Terranism?

The ghosts of Marcant and Maxsym looked equally thoughtful to her, but without being able to see their faces, it was only a feeling.

They arrived at another door at the end of the long room and moved on.

Beyond the door, large red spheres lined one wall. Each machine was perhaps a meter or so in diameter. Red and green lights blinked at intervals along a black strip at the top.

Telisa wondered about the purpose of the machines, but she kept up a good pace as she strode past them: as much as she loved learning about aliens, she wanted to find Magnus. Time could be of the essence.

The room ended. Instead of a door to the next outside section, there was only a hatch leading back into the hallway. The three Terrans sneaked through that portal and returned to the circular corridor.

Telisa hesitated.

This level doesn't feel like a place where I might find prisoners...

She turned to her team and pointed upwards. Marcant nodded. She supposed that if there was an elevator, it might be near the center of the deck. Otherwise, they would have to crawl up a rovling tube.

Time is important.

Telisa headed toward one of the straight corridors that joined the circular one, hoping each of those led toward the center. She started to kneel at each rovling tube to see where it went. Sure enough, more than half of them led at various angles up or down. Those that rose or dropped precipitously had many of the ridges she recognized as providing traction for the rovlings.

Telisa found one that went almost straight up. She crawled in far enough to see if there were any rovlings in the tube. The inside was dark, but her host-body eyes could see the far side, unobstructed. She crawled in and started up rapidly, leaving Maxsym and Marcant to follow at their own pace.

As she shuffled up the tube on hands and knees, she questioned her decision. It was dangerous to take such a tube being used by rovlings. If she came up to one, what would she do? It would detect her presence if it tried to walk through her. If she destroyed it, would it send a death rattle transmission to be picked up by the ship? If not, would she have to hide the remains?

We don't have the time we need. It's worth the risk.

The tube emerged into a very large chamber. She exited the tube and stood, staring in awe.

Rovlings. Hundreds of them lay folded against the walls. Thousands.

Telisa froze. She held up one arm to halt Marcant and Maxsym behind her, but they had not even made it to the end of the tube.

There were at least six rows stacked atop each other on each side wall. Telisa felt nervous to enter such a clearly dangerous place.

If it gives me pause, I bet Marcant is freaking out right now, if he's looking at my feed.

Telisa decided she was not being fair to her once-delicate teammate. Marcant had proven himself in enough dangerous situations now that she should no longer think of him as the skittish hacker-scientist he had once been.

She stepped forward. Nothing stirred.

Telisa resolved to just calmly walk through the sleeping hive of machines and take the next door out. She looked back to make sure the other two were still with her. Marcant stood close behind her—perhaps too close?—and Maxsym was just straightening up from the tube.

Telisa marched them forward. The chamber curved with the section of the ship, but Telisa thought it might be the only chamber on the whole deck. Finally a walkway broke right, toward the center of the fuselage, so she followed it. She saw that each of the six stacked rows on the inner wall were about ten rovlings deep. She suppressed an animal shiver and focused on the hatch that became visible ahead.

They exited into a normal Rovan hallway, albeit a short one. Telisa breathed a sigh of relief. Marcant actually bent over, putting his hands on his knees. Maxsym's ghost shook its head.

Telisa's frustration rose. They had mapped out a fair portion of this deck and the one below, but it was only two of many levels on the kilometer-long section of the ship. Also, there were three other long sections just like this one, plus the even-longer central spine that joined them all together. It was likely Magnus was not even in this section.

She thought about the chances their team members would be on the same level as the rovlings. On one hand, it seemed like a massive rovling barracks, not a place to keep or examine prisoners. On the other hand, if a Rovan was going to keep prisoners, surrounding them by thousands of rovlings would be understandable.

I need to take a risk, but Maxsym and Marcant don't need to take it with me.

"There's no way we will find them in any reasonable time unless we risk communication. I'm going to separate from you two and unstealth, then see if I can contact them. Remember, if you get cornered, make sure you have energy left for your force field. If Adair is right, it might prevent you from being killed," she said.

"Is it really a good idea to split up?" Marcant complained.

"When I send out an active signal, I'll be revealing my presence. It would be better if only one of us takes this risk."

"Why you, then, may I ask?" Maxsym asked.

"I can move faster than either of you. Jump higher. I'll be the best equipped to lose any pursuit, if they come after me with tracker rovlings."

Marcant and Maxsym seemed to accept her explanation.

"There's an alternative," Maxsym said. "We could split up. One of us travels aft, and one toward the bow. Telisa would move through to the spindle and scout the way into one of the other sections."

"That is already partly my plan. I was going to head toward the center before trying to contact the others, to make sure I would be able to get through to them, whichever of the four main sections they're in."

Maxsym nodded.

"Both plans, then. Marcant and I will split up and head in opposite directions from here along this section."

"Then how will we know whether or not to rendezvous? And where?" Marcant said. "I say, we hole up in one of these rooms. We can deactivate our stealth to save energy. If you don't return with the other's location soon, then we'll assume you were captured and proceed without you."

"Copy me your latest door-cracking suite," Telisa said. "If I'm not back in four hours, then assume the Rovans heard me and I'm on the run."

"If they did hear you, you might as well message us," Marcant said.

"She might not know if they heard her right away. Chances are she would try to contact them, and if successful or not, change location quickly after that," Maxsym said.

Marcant brought his hand up to his head. "Okay, when you send the message, route it through an attendant," he said. "Have it send to all of us: you found them or you didn't. Where they are, if you know. Then send the rovlings on a merry chase after the attendant while you slip away. That way, we'll know the situation. If, for instance, Magnus is in this fuselage or one of the others."

"If I find them, I'll head right for them and you two can follow behind," Telisa said. "If I couldn't get through, split up like Maxsym said and keep searching this section."

Maxsym's ghost shook its head.

"It's an interesting plan, but if the Rovans don't hear you calling to the others, then they'll still see the attendant. You will have needlessly given yourself away," he said.

"Send the attendant alone to the spine. Have it call for the others. If it succeeds, have it broadcast their location," Marcant suggested.

"Can it get through the doors on its own?" Telisa asked.

"Yes, but *it will be seen*," Maxsym insisted.

"Eventually, yes," Marcant conceded. "But the Rovans will likely assume it was one of the others' attendants, one that slipped away and managed to avoid detection for a while. They won't know that there's another team aboard."

Telisa grimaced.

We need cloaking for our attendants. Put it on the tech wish list.

"At least, by sending an attendant to do this, we three can stay together," Telisa said. "Ideally, we would all three go to break out the others, leaving all of us in one place to escape or be captured as a group. Any other way, and we have communication problems, which means coordination problems and extraction problems."

The team had gone through several training scenarios where the team had fragmented to the point that no one knew anyone else's situation and it usually ended poorly. When communications broke down, everyone had to have their own objectives to complete on a schedule with a known exit plan.

"We're still a couple of decks from the nearest spine connector," Marcant said. "We can accompany it that far, at least. Check out the security on the spine hatches. I'll download the suite to all of our attendants as we go."

"Okay then, we need either a rovling tube or a Rovan elevator to go two levels against the ship's spinner," Telisa said.

Marcant pointed at an extra-wide set of doors. "One extra-large Rovan elevator, standing by."

The door slid upwards, revealing a spacious square room. It was empty.

Telisa accepted the gift from circumstance. They entered and let Marcant operate the Rovan machinery. As the lift rose, Telisa thought about any other traffic they might encounter.

Rovlings should use the tubes, unless they have heavy cargo, she told herself. *If a Rovan walks in here... well, I'll be pleasantly surprised.*

No such thing occurred. The elevator whisked them to the target and the door rose.

The new level looked different. The corridor outside was at least half again wider than the one from which they had entered. Telisa supposed it was because the deck connected to the spine, making it a higher traffic path through the ship.

"Here we are," Marcant said. The concourse ahead looked wide open, but Telisa spotted a massive hatch, lifted into the ceiling, that could close it all off in an emergency. They sneaked out, looking for any rovlings.

Telisa told one of her attendants to go down the connector tunnel to the spine and send its message. The team gathered to one side, off the main pathways leading in and out of the fuselage.

"Look at that!" Maxsym transmitted. His ghost pointed at a huge green object across the way. It was a something natural. Telisa thought it was probably an alien plant. A thick gray trunk split fourfold, then again eightfold, to form massive green ovoids at the terminus of each branch. The ovoids were formed by two giant, ten-centimeter-thick leaves cupped together, leaving a dog-sized opening at each end where the leaves did not meet. The entire thing reminded Telisa of a cartoonish carnivorous plant with eight mouths, but the leaf cups had no serrations or interlocking tendrils to make them look dangerous.

"Can I get a sample?" Maxsym asked. "It's likely from their homeworld!"

"No, absolutely not," Telisa said. "We're getting our people out of here."

As Telisa stared at the plant, her sharp eyes caught movement from within one of the cupped leaf pairs. She was immediately intrigued.

"Something's in there," she said.

The others watched for a moment until a rovling came out and walked across the plant into another sheltered cusp.

"It's a natural rovling," Maxsym said. "Those plantlike extremities produce niches for it to hide in... perhaps feed upon. I hypothesize that the Rovan's side ports evolved to emulate those niches and provide the rovlings with an incentive to symbiotize with the Rovans."

Telisa smiled at his comments, though it was sad that she had such a great xenobiologist sneaking around in alien battleships instead of out studying the life of the universe.

They watched the plant for a few minutes until they received the attendant's broadcast.

"PIT team, please respond."

There was only a second of silence, then a response.

"This is Magnus. Who are you? Have you been captured?"

Telisa breathed a sigh of relief.

The attendant responded as it had been programmed.

"This communication has been set up through an attendant to obscure our position. We have a fix on you. Help is on the way. Are there other survivors?"

"Yat and Arakaki were alive. But Arakaki's link has since been pulled. Maybe she's dead. Yat was alive as of a couple of hours ago. I'm out of my cell and I can move around the ship."

Telisa received a data package from Magnus with his link map. Several new parts of the vast ship became mapped in her link. Magnus was in an adjacent fuselage, about two thirds of the way up toward the bow.

"I'll keep an eye out for you," Magnus sent through the attendant. Telisa wanted to reply, but she could not. Several locations appeared in his message. They were marked with long numbers; Telisa quickly picked out Magnus's Space Force service number among them.

She dropped the suggested rendezvous spot on the tactical. It was close to a spine connector on Magnus's section. He must have guessed it might make it easier to get to him from many places on the ship.

"Okay, let's move," she said to Maxsym and Marcant. Maxsym took a step forward.

"Actually, we aren't going to take this one," Telisa said. "If the Rovans heard that, they might be thick here soon. Let's take that elevator up to the next spindle connector."

Telisa lit up her proposed route on the tactical. Though a lot of the way was unmapped, it showed how they might rise ten decks within their current fuselage, take the next connector across, through the spine, and out at a right angle to end up at Magnus's rendezvous point.

"Any Terran ship would notice the elevator being used," Maxsym pointed out.

"Any Terran ship would notice an intruder in any room or corridor," Marcant said. "These Rovans seem to rely upon their rovlings for everything, even detection within a ship."

"We have to risk it," Telisa summed up.

Telisa led the way back to the elevator hatch. Marcant had the plan, so he started the elevator up. As they rode, Telisa checked her stealth device. Her link connection displayed a datapane with its energy storage information. She had seventy-five percent charge left.

She ran diagnostics on her equipment. She felt anxious to see Magnus again.

At their destination, the door rose smoothly. At least ten rovlings calmly navigated the concourse outside in various directions.

Why more rovlings here? Do they know something's up? Suspicious about the elevator usage?

None of the rovlings exhibited concern about the elevator opening. Telisa marched out toward the spine connector, avoiding the rovlings. It seemed hard to believe the ship could be oblivious to their presence now that they had sent messages in the open, but Telisa hoped it was just another symptom of lax Rovan security. A more cynical part of her wondered if the ship was watching their every move to learn more about these new aliens that had fallen into the trap.

The concourse leading out to Magnus's fuselage was wide and well lit. They saw another of the huge Rovan plants and two more wild rovlings living in it. Telisa wanted to be able to tell Maxsym to stop and investigate, but they had to continue.

Where the connector concourse met the next ship section, Telisa slowed. She noticed that despite the rovling traffic they had seen on this level so far, no rovlings were now in sight.

Magnus's link became available for connection. Telisa hesitated. She was connected to the team through the Celaran stealth interface.

"Marcant? If we link to him in on Terran protocols, we'll be giving ourselves away, right?"

"Yes, but he's not cloaked so he's already in the open visually."

Magnus's connection became available on the stealth system.

"Wait—Magnus must have told his cloaking sphere to listen for us."

"I'm here," Telisa sent. "We're stealthed."

Telisa added Magnus's link to their team network so he could see their ghosts. He appeared on the tactical.

"I don't have the power left to cloak, but I have enough juice to communicate through it," Magnus said. "I figured you would come in cloaked."

Telisa ate up the distance between them rapidly, preparing to hug him. But when he came into sight, she knew something was wrong. Magnus held his head high, looking away from her.

"What's wrong?" Telisa asked.

"I'm visible, so we shouldn't give any indication you're here, in case I'm being monitored. It might just be because I can send rovlings away and keep them from reporting me, but I'm not really sure what's happening."

"So how *are* you running around without stealth?" Marcant asked suspiciously.

"I found something in one of the wrecked ships. It seems to be... helping me. It gave me some memories, and I can even command the rovlings sometimes, but only for a short period of time," Magnus told them.

Telisa immediately felt concern.

If something is giving him memories, it could be doing other things to his mind.

She decided to remain alert for any signs that he had changed. Telisa was curious about the memories he had mentioned, but they were still on a schedule.

"How can a ship like this have no visual sensors that would detect you?" Marcant persisted.

"I don't know. Maybe it does and it's just toying with me."

"Or more evidence the ship relies upon rovlings for everything," Marcant said.

"Yes. It fits a lot of what we've seen," Telisa said. "Rovlings making new rovlings. Rovlings moving things around. They serve as workforce, army, and apparently, internal sensors."

"Yat and Arakaki?" Telisa asked, preparing for the worst answer.

"I haven't found them. I talked to Yat briefly. Rovlings came in and dragged Arakaki out, kicking and… cursing. They weren't able to fight back effectively."

"Then that's our priority."

"Yat may be stuck in his cell isolated by a force field, or maybe they pulled his link, too," Magnus said. "I don't think they're dead."

"Any evidence?" asked Marcant.

"I was treated well," Magnus said. "I was put into one of those force field rooms like the creature we saw on the Rovan colony planet. I was given force-field furniture, food and water. I think they pulled her link to study it, or study her."

Telisa put aside her fears that they were dead and nodded.

"Okay, hit me with some ideas. We can wander around at random, but can we do better?"

"It seems like a good bet they're still in this fuselage," Marcant said.

Maxsym took a gray and silver device out of his pack. The cylindrical device had an angled tip with holes at one end and a handle on the other. Telisa had seen something like it before: a Space Force target signature scanner.

"A TSS?" Magnus asked.

"Not exactly. It's just the molecule sniffer part," Maxsym said. "If you can take me where they've been, I might be able to point us in the right direction."

"What? Why weren't we using that to find Magnus?" Telisa asked.

"First of all, it only works if you check someplace a person has been. Second, it's just too slow. We might be able to use it to choose between two corridors, but we can't just follow it along or we'll be moving at a crawl. Finally, Veer suits are made to be almost untraceable this way."

"Then what good is it?"

"You said they fought. If one of them got cut, or dragged along the floor, that could have left traces, assuming they didn't have their helmet and gloves deployed. Maybe all we can get would be a general direction, but even that could cut our search space in half, yes?"

"Yes."

"Okay, follow me," Magnus transmitted. He was looking away from them, still physically pretending to be unaware of their presence.

Magnus led them into the new section of the ship. They moved within the area his link had recorded, which made sense. By the time they had traveled about thirty meters, Magnus threw up a route indicator on their shared tactical.

Telisa's weapon came up as a rovling exited a tube several meters ahead in the white Rovan corridor. Magnus had spotted it, too.

"Go back," Magnus said aloud. "Take another route."

The rovling stopped on a dime, turned, and scuttled back into the tube.

"Neat trick," Telisa said.

"More than a trick. This is control much more sophisticated than we've achieved," Marcant said.

"It never lasts long," Magnus sent to them as he walked. "It's easiest to just send them away unless I need something from them. Sometimes, they don't comply with commands, but it seems like that's only when they don't know how, or don't have permission... I'm not sure."

The team made good time down three other corridors until they arrived at the destination corridor. Instead of a sloped wall on both sides, the corridor had one sloped side on their left, with a vertical wall on the right. The vertical wall had a low door beside Magnus, only about a meter high. Telisa looked down the corridor and saw several other short doors.

"This is what the back side of those force-field holding cells look like," Magnus transmitted through his cloaking device. "This was Yat and Arakaki's cell. There's a translucent window on one of the interior walls, that might be transparent from outside. The interior walls and floor are fields, or at least, they're reinforced by some kind of force fields."

He stood as if examining the door for a moment, then looked for rovlings.

Maxsym's ghost knelt and started to roam around the floor outside the door.

"I have her... nothing of Yat... wait. Yat touched or scraped the door here... probably one of his hands. They're moving... they were taken that direction," Maxsym said.

"This way," Telisa said, taking the lead.

Telisa followed the corridor around a turn and to a four-way intersection. They halted. Magnus stood and looked in all directions as if making a decision.

Maxsym came forward and started to test the floor. Telisa kept a lookout with Magnus as Maxsym worked.

"It's much harder this time," Maxsym noted after a minute.

"Keep trying. I hope they didn't pull them through one of those tubes back there."

Maxsym started shuffling down one of the corridors, then worked his way back on the other side and chose another corridor.

Telisa checked her cloaking battery. It was at a little less than seventy percent capacity.

We can do this.

Her confidence was betrayed by a creeping doubt. Magnus had been exploring in plain sight. Was the Rovan battleship playing with him? Following his moves, learning from him? If so, what would it do if they snatched Arakaki and Yat from its grasp and ran for it?

It was beginning to look as if they had hit the end of the trail. Maxsym was working his way down the last branch. Then he stopped and scanned a spot again.

"This way!" Maxsym said excitedly.

The team followed the branch Maxsym indicated. Telisa led the way to a large doorway on their right.

"Let's try it," she told Marcant.

He did not have to work long. Soon the door opened into a room filled with Rovan equipment. It looked like some kind of lab to Telisa. She saw clear containers, rolls of tubing, cylindrical and spherical vats and rows of machinery in white casings. Here and there flat tables had been strategically placed between the machines. Two rows wide enough for rovlings or Terrans had been left clear to access all the machines, which were placed in rows against the left and right walls with another row down the center.

The team went in. Telisa went right and peeked down the second row. She did not see anything moving. Magnus led the others down the other row parallel to Telisa. She could see over about half of the machines, so she could keep track of them.

"Look!" Marcant said. His ghost pointed. Telisa's eyes followed his arm.

Sitting on a shelf across from the platform, a Veer suit and some Terran weapons had been neatly stacked.

"This has to be hers! Or Yat's," Marcant said.

"That's Arakaki's. Look for another set," Magnus said.

Telisa saw Yat's equipment on her side.

"It's here," she told them. Yat's suit told her its integrity was at ninety-five percent, but the top front fastener had been forced. The weapons looked undamaged.

Up ahead, the room ended in a white wall, but two arched openings led into another room, one for each of the cleared paths. Telisa was the first to look inside.

The next room was similar, but less cluttered, and about twenty meters long. On the opposite side, Arakaki and Yat lay side-by-side, naked, on two rubberized platforms. Two other arched doorways opened on the far side, just like the ones they had entered from.

At first Arakaki and Yat appeared to be asleep on their backs, but Telisa's eyes quickly caught sight of silvery tubes leading into the back of their heads where their links should be.

"By the Five," Telisa said.

The others came in the other door. Magnus and Maxsym ran over to them. Telisa ran over to Yat on her side.

"Respiration looks normal," Maxsym said.

"They're wired up. Their links were pulled and now... they're probably in Rovan VR," Marcant guessed.

"Disconnect them," Telisa ordered.

"We can't pull all this. I can't tell how much brain tissue they're intertwined with," Maxsym said.

"Use an ultrasharp to clip it on the outside. Do it now. We're taking them and getting out of here," Telisa ordered.

Magnus sat on the edge of Arakaki's platform and slid his left arm behind her shoulders. Then he lifted her head and torso slightly to expose the silvery lines going into her skull.

Telisa felt a twitch of jealousy. It was a sight she never thought she would see: Magnus holding Arakaki naked in his arms.

Telisa scolded herself for being concerned.

Here we are trying to escape with our lives from an alien battleship, and I'm unhappy that Magnus is seeing Arakaki naked.

Magnus slid his ultrasharp out of its tube-sheath with his right hand and carefully slid it under the wires and tubes. He sliced through them in a second and immediately put the ultrasharp away.

Arakaki's eyelids tightened, then opened. She looked up at Magnus, who offered her a Veer suit. She reached toward him, so he helped her up into a sitting position.

Instead of reaching for her Veer suit, Arakaki grabbed onto Magnus's suit, pulled herself up, and kissed him full on the lips.

Telisa just stood and stared. Even her agile Trilisk-host brain was caught flat-footed.

Magnus's eyebrows rose. He said nothing.

"She's likely confused, disoriented," Maxsym stammered, trying to fill the awkward silence.

"Arakaki!" Magnus snapped. "Get into your suit! We'll get you out of here, okay?"

"You don't want... okay," Arakaki said sleepily.

Telisa turned away.

"Get Yat disconnected," she snapped, then all hell broke loose.

Snap. Pop. Pop. Zing!

"Rovlings!" Marcant exclaimed needlessly.

Rovlings emerged from around the lab equipment back the way they had come. Telisa assessed the threat

142

quickly: it was no random encounter of a few machines that had been on other business; the numbers and sudden appearance could be nothing other than a full frontal assault.

Bang! Bang!

Telisa shot two rovlings in a fraction of a second. She saw another rovling equipped with the sensor module that allowed the rovlings to detect them while cloaked. It seemed to take a moment to Telisa's superhuman reflexes, but her weapon put that rovling at the top of the target queue and fired again, destroying it.

Bang! Smack! Zing! Ka-zing!

Marcant fired on rovlings on his side. Magnus had drawn a baton, presumably because his other weaponry was largely exhausted.

"Get him disconnected!" Telisa ordered, referring to Yat, then charged forward to occupy the rovlings so that her team could comply. Projectiles came in from both directions now, as rovlings came in behind her from two openings beyond the surfaces Yat and Arakaki were on.

Pop! Bang! Bang!

The lab came alive. Rovlings started to flow across the ceiling. Every surface held a rovling, and every nook and cranny emitted projectiles. Telisa felt impacts on her Veer suit.

Thwack. Smack. Pop. Bang!

"Activate your packs!" Telisa ordered. Even as she said it, she realized Magnus's pack was probably empty. Arakaki and Yat did not even have packs on. Telisa kept firing.

We'll be overwhelmed again. We need grenades.

"Go away," Magnus said. "Run away."

A group of rovlings turned and moved out of sight, but others took their place.

"Magnus, can you scatter them?"

"There's too many," Magnus said. "They're flipping back too fast!"

"Group up with the others," she commanded.

"They're down," Magnus said. "All of them."

Telisa did not have time to consider if he meant they were dead or just pinned or unconscious.

We can't win here, and if we keep fighting, they might get hit.

"On me," she said.

Telisa let her PAW dangle by its strap and grabbed a baton and a laser pistol in an instant. She charged down the aisle, shooting and swinging. She cut a path of devastation through the lab while her force field absorbed everything the rovlings had.

Magnus's Veer suit told Telisa he was taking hits. He had deployed his gloves and helmet to protect him.

They burst from the main lab door into a white Rovan corridor, then sprinted off in the direction they had not been before.

Telisa turned and emptied her clip into the rovlings following them.

Brrraambrambrambrrraaaam!

"Send them back! Send them back!" she urged.

Telisa saw a couple of rovlings at the corner turn around. She had shredded the rest, buying them a few precious seconds.

"In here," she told him, pointing at a rovling tube. She had no idea where it went.

Telisa grabbed the edge of the tube, lifted and pointed her feet and slid inside with one smooth motion. Her incredible strength imparted enough momentum to slide several meters, then she pushed herself on through into another corridor.

When Magnus emerged behind her, she flipped off her force field and switched back to stealth. She dilated the field and crept closer to Magnus to conceal him.

"Doesn't that drain it like five times faster?" Magnus asked.

"Yes. We have to find a hiding spot soon. What the hell happened to Marcant and Maxsym? They had force packs, too."

"The rovlings caught them by surprise. They got hit... without their helmets up."

By the Five. Those incredible minds... destroyed by rovling snipers in an instant?

It was almost too much for Telisa to bear. She told herself that they had not been killed, but it seemed a ridiculous hope. The attack had been sudden even for her with her host body reflexes. She balked, refusing to calculate the severity of the mission's failure.

They crawled out the end of the tube. No rovlings were in sight—yet. They were off Magnus's section map, in unknown territory.

Telisa guided Magnus forward. On their right was a Rovan-sized door.

Telisa told it to open. There was a five second delay that felt like forever. Telisa's cloaking energy dropped rapidly toward fifty percent charge.

The door opened. Telisa hesitated only long enough to make sure there were neither Rovans nor rovlings on the other side, then dashed through. The room was large enough for a Rovan, but not much larger. There were bins on the walls and a tank in one corner. It was dry, but had pipes as if it once held water. Gentle lighting from the ceiling illuminated a second room beyond a hexagonal opening, the same size as the first. It looked empty.

"What is this?" Magnus asked.

"It reminds me of those rooms we found in the mountain redoubt. The beautiful place with all the weird little pseudo-rovlings?"

He walked into the second room and pointed at the floor. "That's a waste receptacle, or a toilet. Whatever you leave there eventually sinks through the field and falls down the pipe. It must have been a Rovan's room. A crewmember," Magnus said.

"Then this is a good place to hide. If the Rovans are all gone, we won't be discovered, and if a Rovan walks in here... then we'll have found them."

Telisa started to grapple with the feelings she had suppressed during their escape. Rising depression flipped into a storm of other emotions. It would be easier to deal with her anger than her sorrow, so she whirled on Magnus.

"What the hell was that with Arakaki?!" she demanded.

Magnus shook his head again.

"I don't know, Telisa. Truth check? I really don't know."

She ignored his offered truth check connection. The anger spike dissipated as quickly as it had risen.

"Okay, I believe you. I gotta say, it freaked me out. Life or death situation or not... I just wasn't expecting... I can't believe we've lost Marcant and Maxsym, maybe Arakaki and Yat, too."

"For what it's worth, I didn't see any blood. Maybe they were just rendered unconscious. We'll get to the bottom of it," Magnus assured her. "When we're out of here."

Telisa was almost afraid to hope.

"Of course."

Chapter 17

Siobhan lay in her sleep web as the *Iridar* crept through the void below lightspeed.

"Please identify yourselves," something said on the PIT channel.

Siobhan frowned. The message ID showed it was from Adair. She was happy to hear from someone on the team, but Adair was not the one she had hoped for. She waited for someone else to respond. Caden stirred in the web next to her.

"It's me, Imanol."

"Ah, you were replicated! That's great. Anyone else I know with you?" Adair asked.

"I got the Twitch Queen here with me. Oh yeah, and I almost forgot. Wunderkind and Fast 'n Frightening. They spend so much time locked up in their room it's easy to forget they're on board."

"We're just avoiding you, Imanol," Siobhan said.

The source of the transmission appeared on the tactical. It was the Vovokan *Iridar*. Their own Terran *Iridar* crept slowly toward the coordinates in the warning they had received, trying not to draw attention.

"Abandon that ship! The Rovan battleship will notice you soon," Adair said.

"How did you see us first?" asked Caden, standing up from the sleep web.

"I knew what to expect," Adair replied. "I have some attendant spies out there and I know the signature of your *Iridar*."

"We have some Celaran ships with us," Cilreth said.

"That's great! Stay stealthed at all costs. Do you have a Vovokan shuttle? Or a Celaran one that can cloak?"

"No…"

"I'm sending a Vovokan shuttle right now to get you," Adair said. "You have to get off that ship."

"Where's the rest of the team?" Cilreth asked.

"On a mission in that battleship. I'll tell you more soon. The priority for you right now is simply surviving and avoiding capture."

The *Iridar*'s tactical became much more complex as Adair fed it new information. A very large object, presumably the Rovan battleship, became visible. Many other tagged objects were visible in another data layer. Siobhan saw they were supposed to be disabled ships.

That's a lot of dead enemies.

Siobhan created another channel with her Terran teammates.

"Could it all be a trick?" she asked them. "Is this really Adair? Should we get on the shuttle and tell him how many ships we have with us? The message we got did say it was all a trap, after all."

"It makes sense that Adair was left behind," Cilreth replied. "Besides, the Celarans have detected something affecting their spinners ever since we spooled them down. That's the trap… the way this place somehow funnels in a wide range of routes between these two star systems and pulls every spinner down so that it arrives here."

"It's an amazing technology," Caden said. "Almost a Trilisk-level achievement."

Imanol grunted. "Looks like the rest of the team met their match. These Rovans may not be as bloodthirsty as some, but we'd best not be messing with them at all."

Siobhan and Caden had grabbed as much as they could carry in the next couple of minutes. They had moved a lot of their spare equipment and weapons over to the Celaran ships, since they had anticipated that the Terran *Iridar* might not be able to conceal itself well enough to avoid the dangers of the trap. They would just be leaving the ship earlier than expected.

They were on their way to a shuttle bay when Cilreth called everyone.

"There are six ships leaving the battleship. Presumably they'll head this way soon."

Siobhan accessed the data on the battleship. It was still too far out for them to learn much. She saw that the six ships were each larger than the Terran *Iridar* but comparable in size to the Celaran cruisers around them.

"We can take them, I think," Caden said.

"The Rovan ships are hard to kill," Adair said. "Still, if you all attacked at once unexpectedly... I think you could do it with minimal losses."

"We see ships leaving their vine," Lee transmitted.

"Adair says that the predator ship out there is sending smaller ships to hurt the *Iridar*," she told Lee.

"Wait until they make a missile launch on the *Iridar*," Adair said. "Then you hit back."

"Why don't we hit them first? Before they can destroy our ship?" Imanol asked.

"They won't destroy it. They'll inject a bunch of rovlings into it," Adair said.

"Oh, is that all?" Cilreth said.

"It'll play into our hands later," Adair said. "I've had a long time to sit here and plan, and I've learned a lot watching previous battles here. When we rendezvous I can explain everything."

"Okay, I'll pass your suggestions along," Siobhan told Adair.

"The predator ships will launch a swarm of sublight tools to attach to the Terran vine. Then you use your dangerous tools," Siobhan explained to Lee. "That way, none of the tools will hurt you. We'll let them have the *Iridar*."

She was proud of the Celaran flavoring she added, though the translation service was so good by now that she was wasting her effort.

"How many should we hurt?" Lee asked. The translator put tone on the word 'hurt', making it sound like Lee was already dreading it.

Adair had sent a set of tactical suggestions, showing possible attack arrangements and detailing the time to strike. Siobhan sent them to Lee. She scanned through them and learned that Adair wanted the initial Celaran retaliation to target two Rovan ships with three Celaran cruisers each.

Well, Adair said they were tough. With their mastery of force fields, that makes sense.

Siobhan and Caden arrived in one of the Terran *Iridar*'s shuttle bays. Cilreth was already there.

The tactical showed that the Rovan squadron was indeed headed out on an intercept course for the *Iridar*. She wondered how many other times they had come out to destroy ships that had dropped into their trap. The dead ships were clustered in ways which suggested they might have died together in many groups of six to ten vessels each.

"Do we know who their enemies are?" she asked.

"Were," Adair said. "I think those ships are old. We haven't learned much. Definitely no race like those we've seen so far, with the possible exception of the thing that tried to take over our ship from outside the hull."

That awful thing? If the Rovans have been fighting things like that, then we should try harder to make friends with them.

"Shuttle coming in," Caden warned. Imanol was just walking up to join them. Everyone deployed their Veer suit helmets and waited rather than run back out. The bay detected their preparations and decided it could safely open. The weird bulbous shape of the Vovokan shuttle floated in and settled nearby. The team boarded the shuttle in the depressurized bay in good time. Everyone was eager to get away from the doomed ship.

Siobhan thought about the Terran *Iridar* she left behind. The ship had served them well, but she would not miss it. Nothing had ever topped the luxury of the *Clacker* with a Trilisk AI on board.

Cilreth took control of the shuttle and brought it out of the bay. It felt natural to Siobhan, since Cilreth was their Vovokan expert. She would be able to keep their stealth systems engaged and handle any emergency that came up.

Siobhan watched the tactical. The shuttle crept away from the *Iridar* at a conservative pace. The Rovan ships, on the other hand, were coming in hard. Siobhan suppressed the nervousness that came from watching the shuttle move slowly while their attackers came in quickly. There was a lot more open space around them than the tactical implied, and remaining stealthy took precedence over opening more distance between themselves and the Rovan's target.

"There they go!" Caden said. Each of the Rovan ships released dozens of missiles headed for the *Iridar*.

"This is almost going to be worth it to see those bastards die when the Celarans let loose," Imanol said viciously.

"I've never been so glad space is a big... place," Caden said. Siobhan understood what he meant: they were stuck in a tiny shuttle as the two squadrons prepared to clash around them.

"No missiles have targeted us," Cilreth assured him. Siobhan could see Cilreth was very comfortable with the Vovokan interface. Siobhan felt a little guilty; she had not spent as much time digesting the Terran scientist's information about Celaran tech as she should have. She had been spending a fair amount of time in non-training VR with Caden.

"According to the plan, they're going to strike back about... now," Cilreth said.

They all watched the tactical. It would take several seconds for the light to reach them.

Two Rovan ships exploded. At almost the same time, Vovokan missiles appeared on the tactical, bracketing the Rovan squadron's four surviving vessels. The tactical showed outdated positions of Celaran ships that had revealed themselves by firing.

"Adair sent that salvo of missiles to force accelerations within these cones," Cilreth explained. "That way, the next Celaran salvo—"

"—will have a better chance of guessing where those ships are going to be," Caden finished for her.

Siobhan watched anxiously. Suddenly the missiles went haywire, veering off, correcting, and veering off again.

"Blood and souls, what are they doing? Some kind of hacking?" Imanol demanded.

"I don't know," Cilreth said. "It's too bad. I hope this isn't turning into a real fight."

Siobhan took Caden's hand and squeezed it. They watched in silence as the ships danced.

If Lee's squadron gets cut to ribbons it will be all our fault...

The Rovan ships had apparently lost track of where the Celaran ships were at and were probably unable to re-obtain them. Meanwhile, the Rovan salvo closed on the *Iridar*. The Terran ship's point defenses were not adequate to stop all the missiles... but they did not explode upon impact. It seemed that Adair's assertion about inserting rovlings had been correct.

Siobhan moved to the edge of her seat as enough time passed for the Celaran ships to recharge their rings and fire again.

Two more Rovan ships exploded. Siobhan let out a sigh of relief.

The two remaining Rovan ships returned fire at the nearest Celaran that had revealed its position with the energy emissions. Siobhan kept her fingers crossed.

The Rovan ships turned away and started to run.

"We did it!" Siobhan said.

"The Celarans should press their advantage and finish those last two," Imanol said urgently.

"It's not their style," Caden said. "I'm sure they'll let them go."

"If only we had the *Clacker*," Imanol said. "Then we'd make sure none of them got away."

"We shouldn't be fighting them at all," Siobhan said. "These Rovans aren't like the Quarus. Everyone at Blackhab thinks they're basically not aggressive."

"That may be the case, but this battleship is dangerous," Imanol said. "Those ships came out here and fired on the *Iridar* without provocation."

"At least they didn't blow it up," Siobhan said.

"Is that really much better?" Imanol asked.

"Depends," Cilreth said. "Are the rovlings there to kill everything inside, or just to ensure that the ship isn't a threat?"

"I'm glad we're not in there to find out," Imanol said, and this time, Siobhan agreed with him.

Chapter 18

Yat awakened on a flat table. He blinked once, twice, then recalled that he was on an alien battleship.

Rovan. I'm on a Rovan ship.

He had been dragged here by a group of rovlings. Shortly after arriving in this room, he had been put to sleep.

Yat lifted his head and looked for enemies. His eyes caught no movement. All around him sat large white machines. The machines were silent, but apparently active as signaled by blinking lights on their top surfaces. He did not recognize any of them or their function. They could be Terran machines, but some subconscious cue told him he was in a Rovan lab.

He sat up. He was not restrained—always a good sign. He had only his undersheers on. That detail was less welcome.

Let's get the hell out of here!

Yat scanned the area for his Veer suit. He spotted a Terran PAW across a narrow walkway left for rovlings. He silently got on his feet and crept over to the weapon. His Veer suit was folded beside it.

He grabbed the weapon first and checked it. It told his link that there were only three rounds in the magazine and the laser had a ten percent charge left.

Yat cursed. He set the weapon atop a white-cased machine where he could grab it quickly if need be. Then he went for the Veer suit. It reported ninety-five percent integrity. Yat slipped into it and grabbed the firearm. The flat surface that had held his suit and weapon also had a modified stun baton designed to kill rovlings. He grabbed it and locked its handle onto an equipment slot of his Veer suit. The suit had a stealth orb in a pocket, but the device was just about out of power.

Yat could not remember if he had come to the ship with any companions. He checked the room for other Terrans or Terran equipment but did not find anything. The lab was a long, curved set of rooms, each joined by two arched doors where the two open rovlings paths ran through them. After he explored those rooms, he risked going through a closed door.

A wide white corridor lay beyond. He peeked out. The corridor was empty. He had only right or left as choices unless he wanted to crawl through a rovling tube. He went right and crept along, listening, always ready to cover behind a tube opening if he had to.

He got to a right turn and took a peek.

A Rovan sat in the corridor beyond the corner, lying with its huge shell on the deck. The alien faced his direction, yet Yat's eyes quickly left the creature and focused on another form beyond it.

A tall, two-legged creature advanced on the Rovan from behind. There could be no doubt it was stalking; it strode forward eagerly yet carefully and without a sound. Four tentacles rooted in its main body waved as if preparing to grab the Rovan. Though smaller than the Rovan, its head was much larger than the Rovan's head with a long jaw that looked every bit as menacing as the Rovan's curved mandibles.

Yat feared being spotted but he could not look away. The alien biped leaped atop the Rovan's back in one powerful bound. Yat saw that its legs terminated in single bony spikes rather than any recognizable kind of feet. Yat remained at the corner, transfixed.

What is that thing?! It's nothing like a Rovan.

When the attacker dipped forward and opened its jaws, Yat realized the biped had a different kind of mouth. Its head had opened like a pair of scissors, revealing long ridges of sharp, chitinous material on top and bottom rather than an open maw with rows of teeth.

The creature used its natural weapon to slice through the Rovan's neck, severing its head. Black blood gouted out of the neck stump.

Yat's heart beat so hard it made the carotids in his neck hurt as if they were going to burst. He slid back from the corner, half-panicked.

Calm. But still, run. Just run quietly.

Yat activated his stealth orb and ran. He had already taken four steps by the time he noticed that this stealth had failed to activate. It reported an energy crisis.

He took a peek behind him. Nothing had turned the corner to come after him.

Maybe that thing will stay to eat the Rovan.

Yat had no idea how a scissor-mouthed monster would eat what it had cut, but his desire to survive far surpassed his curiosity. He approached the end of the corridor.

I should probably go several corridors at least, then find a way out or a place to hide.

Yat looked behind again. This time, the biped was visible at the other end of the corridor as it turned the corner.

Its head snapped in line with Yat and lunged after him.

Yat kept running and turned the next corner. He considered his PAW. Should he shoot? He had seen the thing attack the Rovan. Would it be a bad assumption to think it now hunted him?

I don't want to ambush it at the corner, he told himself. *I have the advantage of range.*

Yat's thoughts of where to fight the alien were cut short as he saw a Terran lying against the wall. It was a man in a jet black Veer suit. The man had short, ragged hair, dark beard stubble, and a bent nose. The man remained in place, stiff, with a grimace on his face.

Yat skidded to a halt. He wanted to ask all sorts of questions, but the situation did not allow it.

"There's something coming. An alien that killed a Rovan," Yat said quickly.

"What? What does it look like?"

"Not good. Like a running pair of scissors, except uglier," Yat said. He turned and knelt beside the man and brought up his PAW.

"I can't run. I'm all busted up," the man said tightly.

"I don't have much ammo. If you have a weapon..."

"I don't. Just go!" he said urgently. Then, more resignedly, he repeated himself. "Just go."

"No. Do you know any hiding spots?" Yat asked.

Before the man could answer, the savage biped strode around the corner and spotted Yat. Seeing the massive alien approaching released a new bolt of adrenaline within him.

Yapzers!

Yat told his laser to fire. It released half of its charge at the alien target.

The creature emitted a wheezy scream like a demon horse in pain, but it kept coming. Yat fired again, exhausting his PAW's charge. The creature dodged to one side as if in pain, but no new scream came. Then it was almost upon them.

The man rolled forward into the middle of the corridor.

"Run!" he told Yat. Yat stood his ground and told his weapon to fire a projectile round. The thunder of his weapon was loud in the corridor.

Blam! Zing!

The round ricocheted off the heavy bone of the monster's scissor-jaws. The man was coming to his feet, obscuring any possible shot to the alien's lower body.

"Run you idiot!" the man screamed. He staggered toward the alien thing and collapsed onto one of its legs, gripping it tightly in both arms.

The alien flicked its bony, spiked leg, trying to throw off the man. He fell halfway to one side, then the cutting jaws descended on him. The alien tried to bite the man's arm off, but the Veer suit held, though it compressed too far. The man screamed.

Yat turned and ran again.

You're a coward, he told himself. *But dying is no use, either.*

Oddly, the continued screams behind him were reassuring in that he knew the thing was not running on his heels, ready to snip off his head at any moment. Adrenaline and terror dominated his disposition, preventing any more guilty feelings from taking hold.

Yat considered the two rounds left in his weapon.

It has to have a weak point.

As he ran, he brought up a pane in his PV to edit the target sig. He altered the body zone priorities so that the weapon would send the next shots into a different body section than the round he had already fired into the thing's 'head'.

He came to an intersection and went left to keep out of sight as much as possible. Yat assumed the thing would be coming right after him as it had after killing the Rovan. He would have to face it. It was not a matter of if, but of when.

The corridor branched into a mini-intersection, but there were doors in all three other directions within five meters of the branching. Yat ran toward one, but it refused to open. He looked for any kind of control to use. There was nothing. He turned and checked another with the same result.

Yat heard the sounds of powerful footfalls approaching.

Yat turned in the intersection to face the enemy. He brought up his PAW and told it to fire.

Blam! Blam!

His last two rounds struck the thing in its main body where the two huge legs attached. Yat saw a spray of dark fluid, but the thing kept coming.

Yat retreated down the last branch with the closed door at his back. He dropped the infantry weapon and took out his stun baton. It felt tiny and inadequate. He told the weapon to discharge for Terran nerve disruption rather than the Terran-robotic or rovling settings, even though with an alien, any setting was about equally likely to be effective.

For the first time Yat noticed grotesque holes in the body near the leg juncture. Air huffed in or out of it there. The creature's tentacles feinted toward him. Yat lunged forward to swung at one and missed.

The monstrous creature caught Yat's baton arm in its scissor-jaws and snapped. Yat felt the crunch of bone as though his arm belonged to someone else. There was no pain, though his arm dangled useless.

Yat's Veer suit declared an emergency to staunch the bleeding while Yat tried to roll between the alien biped's sharp-tipped legs and escape.

He had just about cleared the legs when he felt a pinching at his neck. The entire world rolled for a moment as his dismembered head spiralled off on its own. Then the world faded out.

Michael McCloskey

Chapter 19

Imanol bristled as a spindly robot walked forward to greet the PIT team. It was all legs, with a tiny body of clustered attendant spheres.

"Welcome to the *Iridar*!" it said.

"Blood and souls! What the hell are you?" demanded Imanol.

"It's me, Adair. Do you like my new body?"

"Not at all," Imanol said.

"I'm… sure we'll warm up to it," Cilreth said, attempting to sound upbeat.

"Good, because it's an awesome robot body that Magnus made me!"

"Okay, Creep Machine. Whatever you say. So you've been hiding your shiny steel ass in here while the rest of the team is over there on that heavy energy slinger?"

"Exactly!" Adair said brightly, seeming to miss the criticism. "My orders are to stay hidden and wait to assist with the extraction of the team, and if you were to arrive— as you have—then I was to warn you of the danger, apprise you of the situation, and advise you."

"What happened to the *Sharplight*?" asked Cilreth.

"Yeah, fill us in," Imanol said. "What has Telisa and The Machine gotten themselves into this time?"

"The Machine?" asked Adair.

"Also known as Magnus," Cilreth clarified.

"Oh. Well, the team split up—"

"Really?" Imanol interrupted.

"Shut up," Siobhan said. "I want to hear what happened while we were dead… gone, whatever."

Adair paused, then continued.

"There was an argument about whether or not we should revive the Rovan race from a genetic storage station we discovered. The team split into two groups, a group that wanted to find living Rovans, and a group that wanted to prepare for their revival. Though Barrai got stuck on the pro-revive Rovans group with Telisa, Maxsym, and Marcant because they needed the *Sharplight*... and technically Magnus and I were neutral on the proposal."

Imanol shuffled impatiently. He managed to suppress his questions in the interest of getting the entire story out.

"Magnus, Arakaki, Yat, and I arrived here first on this ship. We—"

"Who's Yat?" Siobhan asked.

Imanol snorted in frustration now that Siobhan had interrupted.

"Yat is a new member of the team we found grabbing Rovan artifacts on an old Rovan colony world. He's a resourceful adventurer. It was he who first learned how to bypass Rovan security. He likes to have sex with Arakaki."

"Oh. Got it," Siobhan said.

"When we arrived, we managed to remain undetected. The others went out to learn about these non-Rovan ships. They're all dead and empty, apparent victims of this Rovan trap."

"The trap must have been set up for them, not us," Caden suggested.

"I agree," Adair said. "But the Rovan battleship does not react well to Terrans, either."

"Do you think?" Imanol asked, rolling his eyes.

"Somehow we were detected. Rovlings assaulted them while other Rovan ships started searching for me. They fired weapons, but were unable to pinpoint my location despite several near misses. The team was captured by rovlings. I believe that Magnus, at least, was taken alive."

"So when Telisa showed up, didn't you warn her?" Imanol demanded.

"Yes, but the battleship saw the *Sharplight* right away and sent a squadron to engage it. The second team went in after the others on a rescue mission. A Space Force officer named Barrai died fighting for the *Sharplight*. I tried to save her, but it wasn't possible."

"I'm sorry," Cilreth said. "What happened to... Telisa and Maxsym?"

"And Marcant. I don't know what happened to them."

"You haven't heard anything from them?" Caden asked.

"No."

"So it's Team Three to the rescue," Imanol said.

"Team Three? We're all PIT," Caden said.

"Well, after the argument about whether or not to revive the Rovans, sounds like there was this Yes Team and a No Team. The No Team came here and blew it. They got captured. Then the Yes Team arrived, and went in after them. That makes us Team Three," Imanol said.

"It's not enough to just give us all nicknames. Now he has to name the teams, too," Caden said.

"Okay so what should we do?" Siobhan asked.

"Now we head back closer to the battleship and formulate a plan," Caden suggested.

"We can't just go over there and do the same thing the other two teams did," Imanol insisted. "We have to try something new."

"I actually agree with Imanol," Cilreth said. "And Adair said it has a plan."

"Okay then, Creeper. Do you have any suggestions?" Imanol asked.

There was a pause.

"Oh. Am I the Creeper?" Adair asked. "If so, I think we should hack the rovlings and use them for our own goals. They've proven very formidable along other axes of attack, but we know this is a Rovan weakness, and since all these rovlings are synthetic, it must be a rovling weakness as well."

"Well, why didn't the other two teams do that?" Imanol asked.

"We don't know how yet," Adair said. "It will take some study."

"Blood and souls. How much study?"

"Some quality up-close time without interference from the battleship. Fortunately for us, there are plenty of rovlings out there on your *Iridar*!" Adair said.

"Ah, so this is why you wanted us to wait before we hit that squadron. I had assumed it was so that they would waste their alpha strike on the one ship that couldn't hide anyway," Cilreth said.

"Those were both considerations," Adair said. "If you can grab us just a few—say three or four—and isolate them on the proper frequencies, then we can bring them back here and I can try to perfect our takeover methods."

"With those damn things on our side we'd be unstoppable," Imanol said. "Let's get to it. And while we prepare, you can fill us in on anything else that happened while we were gone that Telisa couldn't put into the official logs."

"Very well," Adair said. "Though that could take days."

"Oh? Been busy have we?" Imanol asked.

"You could say that."

Michael McCloskey

Chapter 20

Maxsym opened his eyes and saw lots of rovlings.

He lay on the floor with a shotgun across his chest. Rovlings crawled over him and more were perched on equipment nearby. He spasmed for a moment, ready to throw them off, then realized that his force field was on and the rovlings could not touch him.

His Veer suit's info pane had an alert in red. It said that he had been injected with a tranquilizer which had been counteracted.

He had been unconscious for four minutes.

Maxsym used his link data to fill in the rest of the blanks. His force field had been brought up by a remote command from Magnus.

Magnus! Telisa!

Maxsym lurched up and looked for his companions. He saw only Marcant, who had started to twitch. It looked like his companion also had his force field active.

Maxsym levered himself up into a wobbly standing position. He saw a low, empty table with a mess of silvery cords draped across it.

Arakaki and Yat! They were hooked up here.

Maxsym gave his surroundings one last scan. He did not see anyone else. The rovlings nearby all faced him, dozens of them, but they did nothing.

They know I have a shield up. But they're not trying to wear it down.

"Ugh. What the hell happened?" Marcant said groggily.

"Rovlings. Lots of them. We're hopelessly surrounded."

"Where are Magnus and Telisa? They would never leave us," Marcant said.

"They must have decided it would be better for everyone if they escaped. We were, after all, unconscious."

"Hrm. Maybe. Why aren't the rovlings attacking?"

"I could only guess. Perhaps because we have force shields and we're not attacking them."

"Then we have a decision to make. We can open fire, blast our way out of here, then activate our stealth and slip away," Marcant said.

"Or we can… surrender?"

"Yes. That's how I see it."

"We could call Telisa for instructions," Maxsym said.

"Yes…"

"Can the Rovans be reasoned with? Can we convince them we just want to leave? Or even be their friends?" asked Maxsym.

"Also: Did Magnus and Telisa slip away? If they're out there, free, then we might be able to fight and meet back up with them."

"There must be millions of rovlings on this ship. We can't win."

"We don't need to. We just need to find Telisa, Magnus, Arakaki and Yat and escape to the shuttle."

"Look at this walkway. There are so many rovlings in here, even if I clear the whole path with this shotgun, the debris alone will block our way out of here. And every time we kill a batch, more will advance."

Marcant walked over to Maxsym's vantage point and looked both ways down the walkway. He saw the scores of rovlings packed into every nook and cranny, the ones lined up on the walkway side-by-side, and the masses of them on the ceiling and perched on every piece of equipment.

"Yep. Let's surrender. I'll tell Telisa and Magnus," Marcant said.

Maxsym set his anti-rovling shotgun down along with a laser pistol and stepped aside. Marcant dropped his own ranged weapons. They both kept their batons on their Veer equipment hooks by silent agreement.

"This is Marcant and Maxsym. We're alive, but surrendering," Marcant broadcast. There was no answer from any other team member.

The rovlings cleared one of the walkways. Then, rovlings pressed forward from the opposite direction.

"Okay then," Marcant said. "We're going this way."

The rovlings forced the two Terrans out into the hallway. Then the entire procession moved through the ship, corridor by corridor. The number of rovlings packed into the passages was staggering. They flowed through the corridors and tunnels like red corpuscles through arteries, stacked one upon the other from the floor to the ceiling. Maxsym half expected Telisa and Magnus to leap out to the rescue at any moment.

They passed a large door on Maxsym's right. Suddenly he was directed to one side and toward the door. But Marcant was being prodded onward. By the time he realized they had herded him onto a different course, he felt like it might be too late to rejoin his companion. He halted.

"They're splitting us up," Maxsym said.

"For interrogation?" Marcant wondered aloud. He was escorted away.

Maxsym walked through the door. It was another lab, similar to the one they had been trapped in, but there were no open doorways on the far side, and less equipment clutter.

At least fifty rovlings entered the room with him, then the door closed.

"We aren't your enemies. Surely you can see that? Our ships are different than those outside... our technology, bodies, language... everything."

"Terran links unnecessarily complex -Rovan demonstrates improvements- situation delta?"

Maxsym recovered from the surprise response quickly. He digested the inquiry. It did not sound at all threatening.

Can this be so easy? They know how to communicate with us!

"You have demonstrated improvements? You wish to in the future?" asked Maxsym. He decided to take a shot at the 'situation' part. "We can work together..."

"Terrans have enemies -Terrans make weapons- situation delta?"

"We do have enemies. The Trilisks have not been kind to us," Marcant said.

"Terran links simple -Terran enemies attack- Terran situation downgrade. Terrans engaged in war -Terrans learn of war- Terran links complex?"

Maxsym thought of the questions in terms of what they knew about Rovans. They had lax security. So the question might be if Terrans had added security— complexity—as a result of war.

"The complexity is partially for security. Is that what you mean? We try to keep our enemies from using our links. Is that how it happened for the Rovans?" asked Maxsym.

"Rovans meet aliens -war ensues- Rovan situation downgrade. Rovans attacked -learn of war- Rovan situation stabilized."

"Stabilized? Good. So your civilization still exists?"

"Terrans meet aliens -mutation?"

"Well, we try to make friends. We've made friends with other races. But some won't… work with us."

"Terrans meet aliens -become friends- situation delta?"

"Uhm, well, we met aliens we call the Celarans. A peaceful race of flyers that subsist upon the sap of huge vines and use very versatile technologies that allow their tools to serve many purposes. We have an alliance with them. We protect each other."

"Terrans meet non-Celaran aliens -become friends- situation delta?"

"We became friends with another race, subterranean creatures we call Vovokans. We could only make friends with one of them, but he has helped us a great deal."

"Terrans meet non-Celaran, non-Vovokan aliens - become friends- situation delta?"

This is definitely starting to feel like an interrogation. I guess I need to reveal less just in case Rovans are not going to be our friends.

"We have encountered others, with mixed results," Maxsym said. "It has varied by individuals involved and oftentimes Trilisks have manipulated the results to their advantage."

"Terrans own many systems -explore- situation delta?"

"We're looking for you. The Rovans. We're trying to find you, but many of the planets we found were empty. You see my force field pack? We learned how to make these from your ruins."

"Terrans meet Rovans - become enemies- situation delta?"

"We'll leave you alone. But we will defend our planets."

"Terrans meet Rovans -become friends- situation delta?"

"We would like to exchange technology. Maybe even make an alliance with you, too... Can I ask a question? Are you a living Rovan?"

"Rovans wanted mind -created this mind- Rovans have effective battleship."

"What are you going to do with us?"

"Terrans in this location -time passes- Terrans in this location."

"Ah, so we... are prisoners here?"

"Rovans capture Terrans -Rovans learn- conversation ends."

The rovlings closed from behind. Maxsym felt a moment of panic.

"Terran in this room -rovlings move Terran- Terran is in new room."

I'm supposed to stay in a cell... wonderful.

Maxsym dutifully marched out under heavy rovling guard. He traveled another forty or fifty meters to a new corridor with one vertical wall and one slanted one. A strange flat door opened upward, and he was forced inside.

Within the small square room beyond, he found Marcant.

"Maxsym! At least you're alive," Marcant said.

"I assume this is our prison," Maxsym said grimly, looking at the bare walls.

"That's a good guess," Marcant agreed.

Chapter 21

Team Three assembled on a shuttle bay deck of the *Iridar*. Caden stood among them, with his full OCP, a laser rifle, and no less than three energized batons. He noticed Cilreth did not have a Rovan pack. She stood facing the others.

"You aren't coming with us?" Caden asked her.

"I'm staying behind with Adair," she said. "I would just slow you three down."

"The shuttle is Vovokan," Siobhan said. "I'd feel better if you were our pilot. When we get there, you could stay with the shuttle. Be ready to get us out of there in a hurry."

Cilreth looked thoughtful, then smiled.

"You got it," she said. "Let me get some equipment."

Caden nodded.

"Don't forget your Rovan pack," Adair told her. "It's critical if you were to get captured."

"Nicely done!" he sent to Siobhan privately.

"It's all true. I wasn't just involving her to make her feel important."

"The shuttle can fly itself," Caden pointed out.

"Yes, but when communications break down, it can be nice to have someone with some experience in control."

"True."

By the time Cilreth returned, Caden, Siobhan, and Imanol were seated in the back cargo area of the Vovokan shuttle, ready to deploy. Cilreth took a seat up front and told the shuttle to get on its way. As Caden had pointed out, it flew itself, but Cilreth monitored everything carefully in case they needed to intervene.

They whisked out into space under cloak.

Caden looked at Siobhan in her seat across from him. Her long legs were tucked between them with her armored knees placed in contact with his own. She was quiet, but did not look troubled. She cradled a PAW. Three attendants nestled behind her left ear, halting their orbits for the time being.

Caden watched the tactical and tried to envision the mission going smoothly.

The Terran ship they had abandoned had been hit multiple times. When Caden examined the feeds under magnification, he saw that it was just as Adair had described. Each hit had embedded a rovling carrier torpedo into the ship.

"Sorry we weren't there to greet you, you little critters," Imanol said. "We're coming to play now."

"Briefly, anyway," Siobhan said.

"We got a plan?" Imanol asked.

"We go into a lock and get their attention. As soon as we make contact with rovlings, Siobhan and I can stealth past the first few," Caden suggested. "Then we'll keep any reinforcements off your back while you capture three of them. With your force pack, you should have no problem absorbing a few hits as you grab them. When you give the signal, we'll turn on our own packs, and we just walk back out of there."

"Simple. I like it," Imanol said.

He can be a real jerk, but when it comes down to business, he's cooperative enough, Caden thought.

"How close?" Cilreth asked.

"Very, please," Caden said. "How about this hatch?" He sent her a pointer, indicating a hatch on the bow where it would be hard to surround them or cut them off from escape once inside.

"You got it," Cilreth said.

"Let's cloak until we're all in there," Siobhan said.

Everyone flipped their stealth on and deployed their Veer helmets. A barrier rose between Cilreth and the cargo section, then the shuttle rear gate opened. They hopped out and floated toward the Terran *Iridar*, mere meters away.

Caden came up to the hatch.

Getting in will be the easy part. Getting out... less so.

Soldier robots came out behind the team, carrying three dark boxes that Adair had assured them would stun and silence the rovlings, isolating them from the others so that they could not be tracked or call for help.

Caden readied his weapon. He signaled the others and told the hatch to open.

Siobhan rushed in before he could even send an attendant to check it. He followed right behind her, leaving Imanol to manage the traffic jam with the soldier robots and the cages.

The lock area was clear. Siobhan looked through a clear portal on the inner hatch. He could tell from her ghost's body language that she did not see anything.

Imanol and the three soldier robots came through in good time with the rovling cages. The outer hatch closed and the lock cycled them through. Siobhan and Caden padded through the lock prep room with their weapons held level. There was no resistance.

They each moved to a flank, guarding the entrance as Imanol and the soldiers came into the room. The familiar lighting of the Terran *Iridar* was operational, showing a quiet, empty room filled with equipment lockers and space suit racks.

Once the entire squad was inside and ready, Caden flipped his weapon to manual operation. They wanted to capture the first few rovlings, not blow them away. If they caught a few of the Rovan machines out by themselves, they might not even have that much fighting to do.

Siobhan signaled them and opened the door to the corridor beyond. She slipped out with Caden on her heels.

The corridor formed a Y just ahead, with both left and right heading deeper into the ship from the bow. No rovlings lurked in the area. Caden's quick sweep of the floors and ceiling did not reveal any battle damage.

"Nothing," Imanol said.

The *Iridar*'s link services were visible to Caden even though his link operated in a passive mode to keep from giving him away. It was tempting to just connect and ask *Iridar* where the rovlings were.

"We'll get their attention in no time. Stay here, Imanol, and we'll bring them in," Siobhan said. Caden could tell she was excited.

The Celarans did a great job of carrying Terran link messages through the stealth connection. Even the emotional inflection metadata comes through perfectly.

"I'll take the left," she said to Caden privately. She flickered into visibility.

"Sure," Caden said on their private channel. "We might as well just send attendants ahead, though."

"They might ignore them. Or just shoot them. It'll take us to get them to follow," Siobhan countered.

Caden laughed. "I knew you would say that."

"Are you two gonna go or not?" Imanol asked impatiently.

"Yes! Caden's getting cold feet," Siobhan told him. She headed down the left corridor.

Caden rolled his eyes and advanced down the right corridor. He sent an attendant ahead to scout out the nearest rovlings and help him avoid getting cut off.

One nice thing about this place is, there aren't any rovling tunnels. One less way for them to pop up unexpectedly.

Caden moved rapidly. His weapon was up, though it was still on manual operation.

It felt strange to play the role of invader in their own ship. With the stealth field on, and his own footsteps completely dampened, he became more aware of the random sounds of the ship. Every noise had become a possible indication of a hostile rovling.

He came to an intersection and stopped. On his left, a ladder led upwards to the next deck, and on his right, a short corridor led to a sensor maintenance pod and a water systems room. He decided at least one of the sounds he had noted was related to the water room; probably the automatic start and stop of a flow through filtering tanks.

He knew he wanted to go forward, but the intersection remained a potential source of flanking rovlings.

I've got my pack and the stealth module. It will be enough to get back through.

He strode on in silence.

"Rovlings in the forward barracks on my side," Siobhan reported. Her transmission went out in the open, which was okay since they were bait at this point.

Caden unstealthed himself and acted on his earlier urge to connect to the *Iridar*. It verified what he suspected: the ship was crawling with thousands of enemies.

Caden noted that she had traveled ahead as far as his own attendant had gone. He was only two-thirds of the way in. The attendant entered an engineering space and saw the rovlings that *Iridar* had reported. Caden scanned them through its video feed.

Looks like the Iridar's automated services have not been compromised... at least not obviously so.

He saw at least a dozen rovlings on the floors and ceiling. Apparently they had not spotted his attendant. One of the rovlings had a now-familiar device attached to its top surface: a detector module.

Why didn't they see the attendant? Maybe they're in some kind of power-saving configuration.

Caden advanced to the doorway, brought up his rifle, and waited.

Any second now, Siobhan will—

The distant sound of weapons fire sounded through the corridors.

"Rovlings inbound," Siobhan transmitted. "A lot of them."

Caden popped around the corner, shot the detector rovling, and turned to run. Though he was now uncloaked, he planned on being cloaked when he returned to the Y intersection. He sprinted thirty meters down the corridor.

The attendant behind him saw that the rovlings had all come to life to pursue him. Then it shot away to catch up with him.

"I have a trap set up on each side," Imanol warned them.

Caden re-cloaked himself and turned to shoot at the intersection near the water room. Rovlings entered the corridor from the engineering space. He ignored the first two in line and started to manually pick off the ones behind, one by one.

At first, he kept up. The two rovlings he had let survive advanced ten meters, then slowed. They could not see him, but the laser rifle pulses kept coming, gunning down their fellows. The pair started to walk in a spiral, checking floor, walls, and ceiling.

Caden still had room, but he was not getting Imanol rovlings for the traps.

"I'm trying to let some through, but they're not moving on," Caden said. "If you come down the corridor just twenty meters, maybe a couple will see you and follow to the trap."

"Try an attendant," Imanol replied.

Caden considered that for a second, then decided that the attendant would just die.

The Celaran stealth orb and the Rovan pack could both be on at the same time, but the stealth effect of the orb was ruined by the force field. Caden activated his pack and then deactivated his orb. He slipped his rifle onto his back and ran towards Imanol's intersection.

Zing. Bang. Bang. Snap.

Rovling projectiles shot in from behind. His field absorbed them harmlessly. Caden did not need his attendant feeds to tell him the rovlings were charging after. And doubtless, behind that group, more had been called in.

Caden got to the angled part of the corridor where it led into the Y and activated his stealth. Then he turned and ran back into the ship.

Back in the straight part of the longer corridor, he saw at least twenty rovlings advancing. They were not spiralling any more, just moving ahead at top speed, which was thankfully slower than he could sprint.

Still invisible, Caden darted to the right around the lead rovling and passed another on the left wall. Then he brought up his rifle and told it to shoot on its own.

Hisssss. Hisssss-is-is-is.

The weapon brought down a sensor rovling down the corridor first that Caden had not even noticed. Then it fired a long series of shots, taking down almost ten rovlings before exhausting its charge. Caden reloaded it. The new power pack fed in from the right side of the rifle, automatically pushing out the exhausted pack on the left and catching it by a plastic line so it would not fall to the ground.

"They're charging through. I'm stopping as many as I can," Caden said.

Hisssss-is-is-is.

His weapon released another series of rapid shots. The emitter aligned itself to any target within a generous cone of fire, alleviating the need to align the rifle for each energy burst. There were still many rovlings coming down the corridor. Caden was sure that the ones he had spotted in the room ahead must have already been joined by others from beyond.

"We have to keep them busy up here," Imanol said. "If they're not fighting me, maybe they'll spring the other two from the traps."

Good. He has two already.

"I'm going visible and falling back to you," Siobhan said.

"Switching to my pack," Caden said.

As he became visible, he had a powered baton in each hand. In two swings he cleared the nearest three rovlings.

Snap. Ping. Bang.

He began to retreat. He took a step, swung, then two steps back. His screen started to draw more power, so that he could see the reserves slowly but steadily dropping.

Caden forced himself to remain calm. The engagement was just like any of their many virtual exercises fighting the rovlings. He started to skip back a little faster, but he did not run away because he wanted to buy Imanol the time he needed to capture some of their enemies.

He smashed two more, then a wave of fire came in.

Crunch. Whack. Pop. Ka-zing! Bang.

According to his tactical, Siobhan was with Imanol at the Y, though her position was at the left entrance to screen him. They were actively fighting several rovlings.

"I have all three. The soldiers are down, though," Imanol reported. "We have to carry the cages."

"Withdraw!" Siobhan called.

Caden was happy to hear the signal. He finally caved to his instinct to run from an overwhelming number of enemies. He gave up the losing battle and rushed back to the Y in the corridor, crushing rovlings on the way.

Thwack! Smash.

At the first intersection he saw the three cages, partly obscured by dead PIT soldier machines and smashed rovling parts. Imanol waded through it, pulling one cage clear and shoving it toward the door to the lock prep room. Then he went through.

Caden ran up and put his batons away. He picked the cage on his side of the Y. He instinctively held it in front of him to screen against incoming fire then realized he had it backwards. He was still protected by a force screen and the cage held precious cargo. He reversed his position to protect the cage.

Siobhan pushed her cage back along the floor with her legs while shooting a whole clip of projectiles down her side of the Y.

Ratatatatat.

Imanol had already run through the prep room with his cage and entered the airlock.

"Any day now kids," he taunted.

Caden lugged his cage to the prep room door. While Siobhan cleared some debris and moved her cage over, he pulled his rifle from his back and emptied its last charges into three rovlings behind her.

Hisssss-is-is-is. Hisssss-is-is-is.

"Grenades," Caden said. Siobhan nodded. He told a grenade to release and sent it down the corridor. Siobhan's grenade dropped from her belt and spun off toward her side a split second later. Then Caden slipped inside with his cage, and Siobhan did the same. Caden sent another grenade through the door for good measure.

Ka-boom! Ka-boom!

They each picked up their cage and ran for the lock side by side.

Ka-boom!

His first grenade reported five kills, his second, six kills.

"You first this time," Caden said.

Siobhan gave him a dirty look, but she knew he had been the first to retreat into the prep room, so now it was her turn. She went into the lock rather than argue at a critical moment.

Siobhan thrust the meter-long rectangular cage ahead of herself and joined Imanol. Caden saw another grenade accelerate out of the lock under its own power, probably one of Imanol's. His Rovan pack said he still had thirty percent of its charge left.

Ka-boom!

Caden dove into the lock, slightly out of control. Siobhan was ready. She deflected him to keep the cages from smashing into each other. The lock door dropped, and Caden relaxed, drawing deep breaths. His Veer suit's helmet deployed as the pressure in the lock started to drop.

"Get back!" Siobhan barked. She yanked him toward the outside door.

"What?"

"Bombardier!"

KABOOM!

Caden watched the walls of the lock crumple away. There was a flash of something fusing with the last of the oxygen in the sparse air, then he tumbled away into silent space.

"Well... that's one way out," Imanol grunted on the channel.

Caden lost control of his cage, but it bounced off Imanol's force screen and back toward him. Caden tried to orient himself and check the integrity of the cage at the same time. When that did not work, he told his attendants to take him to the shuttle while he checked his readings.

Caden's force shield was in the red with less than five percent charge left. His attendants got his spin under control. He pulled out his laser pistol and shot into the ragged hole in the side of the *Iridar*.

Siobhan actually laughed on the team channel.

"That bombardier rovling almost fragged our packets!"

"Rattled your brains, is what it did," Imanol said. "Get into the shuttle."

Caden and Siobhan wasted no time following Imanol's suggestion. The shuttle door closed and Caden flipped off his Rovan screen with almost no energy left.

"We're home free now," Siobhan said. "Just make sure none of them hitch a ride back with us."

"You realize if these things are still in contact with that battleship, it will be used to track our location," Imanol said.

"Yes. Be ready. If we suspect it's giving us away, we vaporize the sucker," Caden said.

"My cage says it's intact," Siobhan reported.

"Once we learn what we need, we should destroy them no matter what, before we go into the battleship," Cilreth clarified.

"Good idea," Caden said. He checked his cage again. It told his link that it was functioning correctly. A sensor inside the cage showed that the rovling was not moving.

Cilreth took them away quickly.

Surely it can't track them? We have both the isolation of the cages and the shuttle's stealth working for us.

He traded looks with Siobhan. She was biting her lip, thinking the same thing. He smiled. Siobhan enjoyed danger that she could directly fight or struggle against, but she hated the dangers that she could not actively avoid or fight off. Sitting around waiting to be picked off inside a spaceship was something she dreaded just as much as the rest of the PIT team.

The adrenaline of the mission was half drained away by the time Caden emerged from the shuttle on the *Iridar*.

"We'll leave your presents on the bay deck," Imanol told Adair. "Mine may be a little banged up. I hope that's no problem."

"Mine's purt near spiff," Siobhan said. "Yours?" she asked Caden.

Caden smiled. "Slickblack, front and back," he reported.

"Puh-leez," Imanol said. "You two know your Core World slang went obsolete about a week after you left Earth, right?"

"Well, there's retro, and then there's *stone age* retro," Siobhan said, pointing at Imanol.

"Stone age? What does that even mean?" Caden asked her privately.

"Not sure," she responded. "For some reason it means really old. Maybe like, so old you became petrified like a fossil?"

Siobhan and Caden left the shuttle bay hand in hand. They walked to Caden's room. Inside, lights snapped on to reveal his Spartan quarters.

"Well, that was pretty tame," Siobhan said, dropping her Rovan pack in one corner.

"Walk in the park," Caden agreed. "The next step is up to Adair."

"Yeah..." Her face lit up. "Let's go virtual and do something exciting. With the pain settings at one hundred twenty percent... you know, to make it feel more dangerous."

Caden smiled back.

She's going to be the death of me... again. But she's worth it.

"I'm in."

Chapter 22

Telisa paced in the Rovan quarters. The need to come up with a workable plan to liberate her team was a crushing weight on her shoulders. At least they had confirmation that Marcant and Maxsym had survived.

Magnus watched her as he wolfed down a striped protein and carb bar from his backpack.

"Our very own luxury suite on this massive Rovan ship, and we have to be on a mission," Magnus said idly. Telisa flashed him an angry look.

"What?"

"You *know* what. Our mission is a complete failure and it's up to the two of us to get it back on track. Don't joke. Think," she said.

"Our people are *alive*," Magnus said. "Think about that. If we make a super aggressive play, will it cause the Rovans to start killing us?"

"Alive for what reason? To run through virtual torture?" she said, but she took his point.

What's our next move?

"What do we have going for us?" she asked aloud. "Stealth. Force fields. As long as our equipment has energy, the rovlings can't stop us. We just need to gather everyone together and make a run for the shuttle. Somehow."

"There's also this artifact," Magnus pointed out. He took out a cylinder that fit snugly in the palm of his hand. Telisa saw that one end was flared, while the other end came to a dull point. It glowed slightly.

"Is it emitting dangerous radiation?" Telisa asked, though she knew if it was, Magnus's Veer suit would probably have warned them.

"Not that I can tell. It implanted some memories in my mind. I think it's been helping us."

"It lets you control rovlings?"

"For a time. It's like it can hack into their minds and insert some commands, but then they go back to normal when the commands are done."

"Or maybe it takes the rovling over but the battleship periodically resets them," Telisa suggested.

"It really only works in small groups. Like no more than… four or five at a time."

"Can it open doors like we can? Could it hack the whole ship, get it to drop its force screens, or turn off the spinner dampener?"

"I don't know what it's capable of."

"Ask it to tell us where our friends are," Telisa said.

"I've asked for all sorts of things, but it's usually only the rovling commands that have an effect," Magnus said, holding the artifact out before him. "It glows when it likes something, or at least, when it can charge up."

Telisa saw the artifact had a dull glow to it, but the glow was not changing much as Magnus carried it around the room.

"It glowed when I put it close to the force fields. Maybe I can charge it up with my pack," Magnus said.

"No, we need that energy."

Telisa kept pacing.

"Wait. It left me something," Magnus said, staring off into space.

"It's talking to you?"

"No… but communicating, maybe. I thought about wanting to know where to go to find the rest of the team. Now I remember a room. An important place, here on the ship."

"But it's not a real memory," she prompted.

"This place is the key," Magnus said.

"What place?" Telisa asked. "Magnus. Is that even still you?"

Magnus looked at her. "I honestly believe it is. But of course, it would be hard to prove I haven't been rewritten in some way."

"How is the place important? The others are there? Or is it important to our escape?"

"I don't know, but I think it might be. Why compel us to go to this place if it can't help us link up and get out of here?"

"Well, for starters, we might go there and then this thing explodes. Maybe it's just an incredibly diabolical AI bomb sent to destroy this ship."

Magnus raised his eyebrows. He did not try to argue that it was too small; the capabilities of alien technology could be surprising.

"Your open-minded creative thinking can really get dark, can't it?"

"I know we don't have many options and we can't ignore this information from a potential ally. I'm just considering various angles."

He nodded.

"We can go search for our friends at random, or we can go to this place," Magnus said.

"My first impulse would be to focus on our friends, but given that we just failed at more or less exactly that plan, let's try what our apparent ally has in mind."

"I'll put it into our map."

"My stealth sphere has almost a half charge left. We need to transfer some of the energy to yours," Telisa said.

"If we were back at Blackhab or the *Sharplight*, maybe we could," Magnus said.

Next time we're back at Blackhab... if we ever make it back... I'm going to get someone to figure out how to transfer the energy between any of our packs and our orbs.

Telisa handed her stealth orb to Magnus.

"I don't need it," he said. "I have the artifact."

"If they come after us, I can run faster and longer," Telisa said.

"I've shown that I can escape. If you—"

"The battleship has to be pretty smart. It'll figure out what you're doing and lock you up for good, or put the cables into your head."

Magnus was still reluctant to take any of her equipment.

I hope we don't all already have cables in our head. This might not be real.

"Leave your Rovan pack here. Take my orb or my force pack," she said.

"I'll take the pack," he said. "But you take mine. Even two percent power can save your life if you surrender."

Magnus disconnected his force pack and traded it for Telisa's.

"Say goodbye to our luxury suite," Telisa said. "We're headed back out."

Chapter 23

Siobhan stared at the captive rovling in its transparent cage. Though she knew the machine was isolated and trapped, she still felt the thrill of danger standing near it. She stepped closer and marveled at its details. It was a masterpiece of engineering.

Magnus had incorporated a fusion of Terran and Vovokan technology in his buglike soldier robots to give them superior strength and endurance. In contrast, the Rovan machines were lighter, more agile, and more graceful. They had no real armor, but with superior numbers and equal or greater firepower, it did not matter.

"You're not going to let that thing out, are you?" Adair asked. Its spindly body was parked across the room.

"Why would I do that?"

"You *like* danger," Adair said.

"Just focus on hacking it. I can get my fix when it's time to go find the others."

Siobhan walked around the cage. The rovling inside rotated to face her, though it had four visual sensors placed in tiny holes ninety degrees apart, just under the lip of its oval body's outermost rim. She wondered if its rotation to match her location indicated an aggressive disposition or merely an attentive one.

"We should give one to the Celarans," Siobhan told Adair. "Their scientists will be able to help us."

"Sure. Send one over," Adair said.

"So easy to convince you…"

"Well, to be truthful, I told you I needed three just to make sure I would get the one I really need and a backup."

Siobhan grimaced.

"What if we had died trying to get that third one?"

"I trust in your skills. Besides, like you said, the Celarans could learn from one."

Siobhan rolled her eyes. "See if we trust you again," she said.

Siobhan almost suggested that Cilreth take a rovling to the Celarans, but then she remembered that Cilreth was helping with the hacking because she knew the Vovokan computers so well.

Caden and I are the most familiar with Celarans, anyway.

She poked Caden on a private channel.

"What's up?"

"Wanna go on a milk run?" she sent Caden.

"With you? Sure."

"Meet me at the shuttle in ten. Bring your OCP."

"OCP? Milk run, huh?"

"Well, I heard you're into that whole safety thing," she teased. "Besides, fully equipped, if anything happens we'll be ready to kick it."

"I wouldn't dream of leaving without it."

Siobhan called a couple of soldier robots to carry away one of the rovling cages.

"Another thing…" Adair said.

Siobhan looked at Adair. It did not feel like she was looking at the physical body of an intelligent being. It was like talking to a robot that was remotely controlled by a person named Adair.

"We need to interface this *Iridar* with the Celaran-stealthed communication systems," Adair said. "The Vovokan stealth capability is almost as good as Celarans', but we have no real way of communicating our precise positions to each other. We could actually collide and do serious damage, not to mention, reveal our positions."

Siobhan frowned and wondered if Adair was simply trying to delay her.

"Collide out here in interstellar space? Seems very unlikely," she said.

"Well, yes, it would be if we just moved randomly about. But we might each calculate the same optimal positions to take up relative to Rovan targets. Anyway, collide or not, we need to coordinate smoothly," Adair said.

"Okay, I'll mention it."

"Thanks!"

Siobhan followed a procession of four PIT soldier machines, two of which carried the rovling's containment box on their low backs. She had thought that Magnus's machines movements were lifelike before, but after seeing so many virtual and real rovlings, the PIT machines looked heavy and slow.

Caden was waiting when the group made it to the shuttle.

"You're usually not so slow," he commented.

Siobhan threw a hand out in a flourish, indicating the soldier bots.

"It's my entourage, okay? We're taking this rovling to the Celarans so they can help study it incarnate."

Caden shrugged. "Okay…"

He's wondering why they can't just study it remotely.

"I think the Celaran scanners may be better than Vovokan ones. Well, other than mass sensing, of course. Besides, this will let them do their own experiments as the ideas emerge."

"Hey, if we gotta, we gotta," he said.

They boarded the shuttle and left the *Iridar*. The area of the Rovan Trap was fairly quiet on the tactical. The *Iridar* held station relative to the Rovan battleship, the Celaran squadron, and the ruined hulks of alien ships.

Siobhan shook her head. The tactical looked so *wrong* without a star dominating it.

We're so far away from anything out here.

"How did the Rovans even think about doing something like this? Why didn't they just put this battleship at the system they wanted to protect?" she asked aloud.

"Surprise," Caden said. "Their enemies' spinners come down unexpectedly in interstellar space. They're not ready. They get cut up without a chance to coordinate or sneak into the protected system."

The shuttle closed on a cloaked Celaran ship and slowed for rendezvous. Siobhan and Caden let the two vessels attach to each other using a super-adaptable Celaran airlock. Then they walked in to meet Lee.

Like most Celaran ships, the inside of the vessel was a large open space without decks or sealed off rooms. Alcoves littered the inside surface in all directions.

This is a terrible ship design to take into combat. But they probably wouldn't be taking them into combat if we hadn't asked for their help.

As Siobhan stepped up under the light gravity that settled her against the inside of the hull, a Celaran shot out from a nearby alcove, headed directly across the inside of the vessel in a blur.

At least a dozen Celarans lit their bodies enthusiastically. At first Siobhan thought it was for her and

Caden, but then she saw that a group of them were lined up on the far side. They did not seem to be paying attention to her.

Lee flitted up beside her.

"What are you doing?" asked Siobhan.

"It's a game!" Lee said. "You wait until you can spot the other team's ball. Then you leap across as fast as you can and try to grab it from them. If you catch it, you can fly back to your team and gain a point. If you miss, then you stay over there and become part of their team."

"It's a good thing I'm not playing," Caden said. "I can't see the ball."

"It's hidden," Lee said. "It would be *much* too easy otherwise!"

"We brought you a rovling. Please be very careful with it! It's dangerous," Siobhan told Lee.

"We're scared. But we'll study it," Lee said.

After your game! Ha!

"It can't get out of the box," Caden said. "But if it somehow did... do you have any tools around to take care of it?"

"I have my PIT tool rods," Lee said. "I can take it apart with a laser tool. Or make it fly apart with the exploding tools."

"Good," Caden said, smiling.

"We want to watch your game a while," Siobhan said. "Then maybe we'll try it out."

***

Ratatatatatat. Ratatatatatat.

Siobhan let loose a full clip at a dense group of rovlings. Their fragments skittered across the white floor, emitting wisps of smoke.

The simulation was loud and frantic. Team Three was learning how to hack rovlings in high-pressure situations. Siobhan's role at the moment, however, was just to kill the ones getting in the way.

Ratatatatatat. Ratatatatatat.

Siobhan fell back behind her cover, a carbon support beam. She checked her tactical. Their rear watch attendant had not yet reported any flanking forces. Imanol worked ten meters behind Caden and Siobhan, securing the flank and directing the PIT soldier bots to take over rovlings by replacing key parts of the Rovan software.

The team did not know how effective their rovling hacking might be, or how long it might take, so the rules of the simulation had been set conservatively: they would have to target and "infect" rovlings using PIT soldier robots that had been equipped with special comm modules that could interact with the rovlings. Such soldiers had no additional cargo space, but the trade-off seemed worthwhile.

Caden cycled another rocket into his launcher and signaled his readiness.

She nodded to him and put her weapon around the corner. It fired a half clip down the corridor, trying to cover for Caden. Cover fire was not as effective against rovlings as it was with Terran opponents; the rovlings did not particularly care to duck and cover when they charged down the corridors. Still, the fire killed a few and gave the others another target to shoot at, so it was of some limited value.

Whoosh! Ka-Blam!

"I have some connections," Imanol said. "Keep an eye out."

Siobhan's attendant darted out and gave her a feed of the corridor. It was again filled with rovlings. Three of the rovlings made sharp turns and climbed up the wall, then onto the ceiling and held their positions. By previous agreement, Siobhan knew these were under Imanol's control.

"I've got five of them," Imanol announced. Siobhan did not know where the other two were, but she took it in stride. Things like this always happened in battle.

"Save them up! We need ten at least, to make it across the open space at the end," Siobhan said.

"I'm not sure. There's more coming all the time," Caden said.

"I'll get what I can in the next minute, then we go," Imanol said. He was the acting commander of the mission scenario, so Siobhan prepared to move out.

Caden loaded another rocket. He took a moment to tell it where to explode so that it would not destroy their own machines. A few more seconds ticked by, then they popped out in tandem.

Whoosh! Ratatatatatat. Ka-Blam!

"Okay, cease fire…"

Siobhan went back under cover and waited. Long seconds passed. Siobhan forced herself to a calm she did not feel. More rovlings had to be coming, and they would be surrounding the team soon.

"I have fifteen! Move out!"

Caden and Siobhan emerged from cover. Siobhan's tactical showed her which rovlings they controlled and overlaid green onto them in her vision. Her weapon added the rovlings under their control to its friends list.

The objective lay beyond the open area at the end of the corridor, past a series of rovling tubes and a force field. If this was like other scenarios they had challenged today, there would be a generator out of sight that could be disabled with a breaker claw, which meant they had to dominate the open space for at least ten or twenty seconds to break through.

Caden let his last grenade roll ahead amid a group of friendly rovlings to distract fire away from it. The team's rovlings opened fire on the enemy ones, catching them by surprise and getting six kills before return fire came in. The grenade accelerated into a side room and exploded.

Ka-boom!

The grenade reported only two kills, but it had seen the generator before detonation. Caden and Siobhan sprinted out of the corridor toward the generator room.

Imanol emerged behind them, using his screen to protect a PIT soldier bot.

Siobhan's screen took a big hit as she crossed the space. It told her there was some specialized rovling in sight that could do a lot of damage. She let her attendants try to spot it while she concentrated on the current task at hand.

She burst into the generator room. Rovlings crawled over large pieces of Rovan equipment inside. Siobhan kneeled, then accessed her breaker claw and told it to start wrecking the machines inside. Caden did the same on the other side of the doorway.

Kaboom!

What would have been a dangerous explosion became a harmless fireworks display in a Veer suit behind a Rovan force field. Siobhan and Caden spent no time celebrating; they knew time was tight. They each rotated around the edge of their side of the door and checked on the battle outside.

The Rovan atrium was filled with rovling fragments. A pile in the debris had once been a PIT soldier bot. Imanol was across the room with his back up against a wall. Just as Siobhan looked, the six-legged soldier machine behind him shattered to pieces.

Imanol's force screen was still up. He pointed over toward Siobhan.

"That's our last one! Protect it!" Imanol said.

Siobhan was four meters from the soldier. It was tucked into a niche at knee-level. Caden ran by her toward it.

"We might make it from here," Siobhan said. She was itching to charge the objective.

Imanol looked angry for a moment, then he nodded.

"We can't capture many more with just one, anyway. I'll leave it here to try and cover our rear."

Three green rovlings rotated to face the way they had come as Siobhan ran by. As expected, the force screen protecting the large opening leading to the objective had died down.

The tactical showed that seven rovlings fought on their side, but one by one they were destroyed by the Rovan ones.

Siobhan decided to spend the last of her ammo on every rovling in sight and hope for the best. She still had twelve percent energy in her Rovan pack and two stun batons at her belt.

Ratatatatatat. Ratatatatatat.

The objective lay just ahead. She tossed her spent weapon aside and sprinted for it. Caden was by her side. A landcar-sized machine had the objective tag on it. Siobhan took out her batons. They came toward the end of the connecting corridor. There were blind spots to the left and right, but the objective was only five meters beyond the end of the corridor.

Just as Caden and Siobhan reached the end, a bulbous rovling scuttled out in front of them.

A bombardier.

The simulation ended for Siobhan in a bright flash.

She opened her real eyes on the bridge lounge where she had connected to the scenario. She slammed her fist into the pliant arm of the lounge.

"Frackjammed packets shoved up my slippery silver slit!!!" she said, hitting the arm with all her strength.

She realized that Adair waited nearby. Caden had been ejected from the sim at the same time, but Imanol remained a few moments longer. She felt glad for that, because otherwise he would have had a comment on her colorful language.

At least he can't complain about the charge. He told us to go for it.

The way the soldier bots carried the equipment that suborned rovlings invalidated a lot of the previous PIT training: the soldier robots were supposed to be there to die in her stead. The new role caused a reversal of priority in their tactics; suddenly the soldier robots were no longer expendable. Though they could sacrifice one or two with little degradation in effectiveness, they needed to keep some alive throughout the mission.

The team had been working for hours on the new tactics. Adair entered the room. Imanol and Caden came out of the sim interface and looked around.

"How was your scenario?" Adair asked.

"It was great. You have something to share?" Imanol asked bluntly.

"Well… yes. I can control the rovlings now, and I know how to spread that control among them."

"Then what are we waiting for? Let's go," Caden said.

"Should we rest first?" Cilreth asked. "Or even run more simulations?"

"'Lutely not!" Siobhan said.

Cilreth looked at Imanol.

"Your suggestion is sensible, but none of us are going to be able to get any sleep short of the drug induced kind anyway," Imanol said. "The sooner we take this new breakthrough to the aid of our teammates, the better."

Cilreth nodded.

"Let's go get them," Cilreth said. Everyone left eagerly to collect their gear.

"Lee's on the channel to finalize our plans," Adair said. "Zhe's standing by to assist."

"Sunny day!" Lee said. Marcant's old translator would have just said 'hi', but the newer translators coming out of Blackhab supported configurations that allowed more genuine Celaran flavor to come through. Siobhan had set hers to work this way to understand the Celarans even better than she already did.

"We're ready to go in and find our friends trapped on the enemy vine," Siobhan said as she walked with Caden to the armory.

"How can we help?" Lee asked. A video feed from the Celaran ship showed the Celaran hovering upside-down, then spinning upright in midair, relying upon a lift rod to stay aloft in the low gravity of their vessel.

"If you reveal one of your ships, then the Rovan battleship will probably send some ships out after it. Then we can slip into the battleship," Siobhan said.

"Rootpounders are ridiculously foolhardy to go searching under a leaf that they know has a lurker beneath," Lee said. "We can show one of our ships, then hide it again, or send it running away."

"You could ambush them, just like we did when they attacked the Terran *Iridar*," Siobhan suggested.

"We're not the danger underleaf. The Rovans are!" Lee said. The Celaran became agitated and flew in a tight loop then darted across the Celaran niche as if hiding. "We will run."

"You've never fought the predators instead?" Imanol asked.

"We fly away!"

"That's their way," Siobhan sent Imanol privately. "It's very ingrained from their origins."

"What about defending your young?" Imanol asked.

"Our young flee too."

"But now you're advanced. If one of your young was threatened, and you could save it by killing the predator, you would, right?" Caden asked.

"On established Celaran planets, the young are kept within the safe zones until they are trained and equipped to fly away very quickly," Lee said.

Caden looked at Imanol and shrugged.

"Well, we certainly welcome your help," Siobhan said. "Your plan will work for us. You show the Rovans one ship, then it cloaks and escapes when their squadron comes out. That's all we need to get in."

"Good," Lee said, emerging from the corner of the niche. "I hope you can save our friends."

"We will," Siobhan said.

Chapter 24

The Rovan battleship was huge. Magnus had wandered through many parts of the vessel, sending away rovlings in all directions. The new path in his PV crossed that known territory and continued beyond.

"You should activate your stealth," Magnus suggested. "It's been letting me wander around the ship for a while."

"If we get in a tight spot, I will," Telisa said. "Otherwise, we have to conserve it. That's just the hard reality of it."

Magnus checked the alien cylinder. It was not glowing. Whatever it was, it had given them this path. It was probably made by the enemy of the Rovans. Would listening to its advice make them the enemies of the Rovans? In general, his impression of the Rovans was that though their rovling minions could be merciless, the Rovans themselves did not seem to have been bloodthirsty creatures.

A rovling wandered out into the corridor before them. Magnus sent it away. He felt some relief that his power over them had not been nullified by the battleship after their recent battle.

"Can you tell me anything else about where we're going?" Telisa asked.

Magnus recalled his memory of their destination again. It was a cold place, a place hard to move in. He saw large hemispheres sitting on their flat sides in a room being maintained by thin, spidery robots.

After that, the memory had no scaffolding to connect it to any other experience he could recall. Such an isolated idea had to have come from the alien artifact he carried with him.

"It's a room with complex red machines in it. A place that is… hard to move in."

"So it could be like… heavy gravity?"

Magnus thought about that for a moment. He snapped his fingers.

"The kinetic dampening like we felt in the space station computation rooms," he told her.

"Aha! So it's data that's so critical to our escape?"

"I don't know. Maybe this thing can take over other parts of the ship from there?"

"Which could land us in even more trouble, depending on its intentions," Telisa said.

"Yes."

Telisa shook her head. "I just want to get the team out of here."

A plan born of desperation… but what is it this thing wants us to find?

Magnus saw something new ahead. A tall, gray object dominated the center of the long corridor. Telisa had already spotted it with her sharp vision.

"It looks metal… square corners… if that's a robot, it's not like anything we've seen."

"I could send it away," Magnus offered.

"No, I want to see it. Over here," she pointed. They moved into the triangular side-space of the corridor and nestled between a rovling tube and a support beam.

"Give me your stealth orb," she said.

Magnus handed her the charged Celaran cloaking sphere. Telisa activated it and dilated it until they were both hidden.

"Stay perfectly still. We need to minimize the drain," Telisa sent him over her link. Magnus knew the orb would draw more power to hide both of them, but since they were crouched tightly together and perfectly still, he hoped it would not be bad.

He heard a smooth rolling sound as the object approached, but from the niche he could not see it until it was almost upon them.

The object was a metallic rack or shelving unit. It looked like a rolling bookcase. Then as it moved along beside them, he saw instead of shelves, the rectangular frame held three rows of four oversized rovling niches. Most of the niches were empty, but three of them held passengers: bombardier rovlings. As it passed, Magnus saw that it was propelled by four normal rovlings, two on the floor and two on the ceiling.

Telisa and Magnus remained still until the procession had moved away.

"Why do you think they were moving those rovlings around in that thing?" Magnus asked over their link channel. "I assumed the rovlings travel everywhere on their own using the tubes."

"Maybe those bombardiers are too heavy and slow to walk everywhere on their own. But it doesn't seem relevant to our mission."

Magnus accepted her answer as good enough. Telisa deactivated the sphere and handed it back to Magnus. He peeked out into the corridor. The carrier assembly had continued to move away and no other rovlings were in sight. They emerged to resume their trek to the mysterious location the artifact had fed to them.

They turned the last corner on their route and got a look at the outside of the objective at the end of a thirty-meter corridor.

Eight rovlings rested on the walls and ceiling adjacent to a heavy-framed portal. A soft red light bathed the entrance. At first, Magnus thought the glow might be a force field over the opening, but he decided the light emanated from the room beyond.

"Can you send them away?" Telisa sent.

"Not eight at a time. The others will likely raise some kind of alarm."

"You could go up cloaked and send them away a few at a time," Telisa suggested.

Magnus knew that the cloaking devices, unless otherwise configured, absorbed whatever energies they might emit to hide them. That included visible light and most radio waves.

"I think the cloaking sphere would absorb whatever frequencies this artifact works on," Magnus said.

"Maybe. Or maybe it uses 'more exotic' means," Telisa said, referring to Marcant's explanation of the propulsion provided by Vovokan attendants.

"I can try if you want," he said.

"They're clustered. One grenade will get them all," she pointed out.

"And alert the ship."

"I don't understand what's going on. It has to know we're here anyway, right?"

"I think the rovlings serve as its internal sensors. It doesn't seem to track things inside by any means other than the rovlings," Magnus said.

Telisa digested that for a while.

"Take my stealth orb—*again*—and see if your artifact can dismiss the rovlings through the cloak. If it can't, then slip on by and check out the room."

"If it can't take over the rovlings from in the cloak, I doubt it can do whatever it needs to do in the room through the cloak."

"See if you can find a spot to hide without the cloak. If all else fails, bring the orb back to me and I'll pop this last grenade on them from inside the cloak."

"Sounds like a plan."

Telisa handed Magnus her cloaking sphere. Magnus activated it and walked toward the rovlings. None of them had any detector equipment on their top mounts: Magnus saw only projectile weapons and one energy emitter.

"Make them leave," Magnus urged. The cloaking sphere dampened his voice, but the artifact would pick it up within the cloak.

As he feared, the rovlings did not comply. Magnus almost took a step to start working his way past them, but he decided to try for a little longer first. He checked the energy absorption readouts of the Celaran orb in his link. Through an interface Lee had built for the Terrans to enable them to fire their lasers from within the cloak, Magnus saw a collection of radiation frequencies and patterns that had recently been blocked from *inside* the stealth shell.

If that was the artifact trying to command the rovlings, then I need to let that through and it will work.

He used the interface to open the field to the energy patterns he had identified.

"Try again. Make them leave."

The risk was worth it. Three rovlings skittered away rapidly. After ten seconds, three more rotated downwards, walked down the wall to the floor, and ran off. He sent the last two away within the minute and sent Telisa the all clear.

"Good to know it works," Telisa said.

"I had to weaken the cloak at certain frequencies and data patterns to let its commands out," Magnus said. "As long as we have it set that way, the cloak won't be perfect. In fact, it's probably sending Rovan style commands on Rovan frequencies..."

"And yet you've been wandering the ship doing just that," Telisa pointed out.

Magnus shrugged. "This artifact may have been designed by an alien spy that knows a lot more about Rovans than we do."

"Maybe. Or the ship has been toying with you. But why?"

"To gain information," Magnus guessed. "To discover our objective."

"If the artifact gives you any ideas about sabotaging the place, hold off. Maybe the ship is waiting for us to prove that we're its enemies."

Magnus nodded.

They walked to the doorway and looked inside without stepping in.

Eight land-vehicle-sized hemispheres of smooth red material rose from the floor. Thick tubes as thick as Magnus's torso connected the hemispheres like vertices between spherical nodes in a graph. Four thin-legged rovlings with awkwardly shaped bodies floated above the assembly, moving so slowly that they appeared almost frozen in time.

The scene struck Magnus as so surreal that he wanted to simply stand and stare for longer, but they could not risk it. Telisa looked at him and tipped her head toward the room.

Magnus took out the artifact and checked it. It glowed weakly.

He walked into the chamber, still cloaked. His limbs started to resist movement. The room felt like a glue trap. He did not want to go very far inside, as it would be slow getting back out.

The room was roughly forty-meters square. From his new vantage point, Magnus saw beams or pipes of the same red material crisscrossing the walls and ceiling. He saw three rovling tubes that emptied into the room near the ceiling and another portal at his level on the far side.

The artifact in his hand flickered. Magnus tried in vain to detect new memories, but nothing came to mind.

Why did we come here? What do you want?

Two rovlings entered from a tube near the ceiling. Magnus sent them away, but others had already started to enter the room from other tubes.

"They're onto us and I can't clear them all," Magnus warned.

"What happened? Did the artifact accomplish anything?"

"I don't know."

Brrraambrambrambrrraaaam!

Telisa started to fire out in the corridor. Magnus retreated toward her. Rovlings poured into the red chamber from all directions. The strange thin-legged rovlings that floated in the middle of the room did not react to any of it.

"More of them! We can't do this," Magnus said.

"Run away. Stay out of prison," she said.

"There's too many—"

"You have the good stealth orb. Take the artifact and go," Telisa said. "Try to find out if it accomplished anything!"

Dammit!

Magnus hesitated one second, though he knew full well there was zero time to dally.

"I'm counting on you to spring me from wherever they put me," Telisa said. "Leave now so I can surrender before my pack is exhausted!"

That drove Magnus into motion. With all the rovlings nearby, Telisa might find it hard to survive until she could activate the almost-dead pack and surrender. He ran down the corridor, leaving her behind.

Dammit. We just can't win this.

Chapter 25

Caden felt ready for action as he waited next to Siobhan on the cloaked Vovokan shuttle. The back of the small spacecraft was packed with PIT soldiers; each and every one was precious. Ten soldier bots would normally fit in the racks above their heads, but they had squeezed in another eight soldier machines on the floor and across their laps.

Caden's mood was bolstered by Adair's assurance that the hacking would take place faster than it had in their practice scenarios. That was mostly good news of course, but it also meant that their expectations from training would be off. He made a mental note to be one tick more aggressive than he had learned to be in the simulations.

The feed from outside the shuttle was ominous. Caden could not help but feel intimidated by the size of the Rovan battleship. At any moment it could reach out and swat them. The shuttle approached within a couple of kilometers of the Rovan vessel and took station.

"Adair. We're in position," Cilreth sent.

They waited. Caden resolved himself to the annoying delay. For him, the real mission would not begin until they stepped off the shuttle. A minute ticked by, then two. He visualized the team going in and taking over legions of rovlings, rescuing the others, and returning with the team stuffed into the tiny shuttle.

Caden saw a Celaran ship appear on the tactical in his PV. Suddenly he wondered if Lee was on the ship that exposed itself to the Rovans.

The seconds ticked by with no response from the Rovan juggernaut.

"This has to work," Caden said impatiently.

'Not helpful' Telisa would say. Be more positive.

"Adair was certain it would," Cilreth said.

"I wonder how many ships it has left," Siobhan said. "It probably took some losses, destroying all those ships out there, and the few we've dealt with."

"Are you implying they might not have anything left to send out?" Caden asked Siobhan privately.

"I don't know whether to hope for that or not," Siobhan said.

Caden considered it as he watched the huge battleship. If it was out of squadrons to sortie, then it could no longer project power across the space of its trap. On the other hand, how would they ever get in to rescue Telisa?

"Here they come," Cilreth said.

Caden internally exulted at the news, though it came with a small dose of nervous adrenaline.

The battleship had opened a massive bay door. Rovan ships emerged. Caden counted four cruiser-sized spacecraft.

Cilreth waited until the first of the ships neared the suspected shield location.

"They're coming through. I'm going for it," Cilreth said.

She started the shuttle toward the battleship. Almost immediately, the shuttle turned aside.

"What? How?" Siobhan asked.

"Rovans must be able to drop the shields piecemeal," Cilreth said. "We need to get closer to the exit pattern of the other ships."

"Hurry!" Imanol urged. His voice betrayed that he was, if anything, even more eager than Caden to get in there.

"Activate your packs!" Cilreth ordered. Caden and the others released their harnesses and activated their Rovan packs. Then they strapped themselves back in.

Cilreth concentrated on her PV. The shuttle shuddered. Caden's body shifted to his left, then his right.

"We made it," Cilreth said. Her shoulders relaxed as the tension drained out of her.

"The ship doors…" Siobhan said.

"Yes. We took too long finding our way in. We're inside the shields, but stuck outside the ship."

Caden heard their words, but it was the sight of the bay doors shutting in a video feed that drove it home. They had failed to get all the way inside!

"What now?" Siobhan asked.

"I guess we have to wait until that squadron comes back," Cilreth said.

"That could be a big chunk of time," Imanol pointed out.

"Then maybe we should find a place to hide the shuttle and break in," Caden suggested.

"This is no sim and it's our teammate's lives you're playing with," Imanol said sternly.

"They could be dying right now," Siobhan said.

"Lookie there," Cilreth said. Caden noted her playful tone. She must have topped off her dose of twitch before heading out on the mission.

"Another shuttle," Siobhan said. "It must be Telisa's."

Cilreth closed her eyes for a moment. "It hasn't been in contact with her since she went in," Cilreth said.

"What's that?" Caden asked. Siobhan saw ghosts play across the tactical. The Rovan shield blocked everything for a moment, then glimpses of the area got through again.

"Adair showed the *Iridar*," Cilreth said.

"Also, the Celarans are attacking the squadron that came out after their ship!" Siobhan said.

"They *are* doing an ambush! Lee must have changed zher mind!" Caden said.

"They're doing it for us," Cilreth said. "Adair probably saw that we didn't get in."

That gave Caden pause. Adair and the Celarans were risking their lives just to get the team a chance to enter the battleship!

If they get us in there, we've got to succeed.

"The Rovan ship will learn," Siobhan warned.

The connection with Adair cut out.

"Starting with bolstering their shields, which has cut our views of the outside," Caden concluded.

"What do you expect?" Imanol said. "Adair and Lee just reminded them that there are a lot of enemies out there. Now, we may never be able to get back out again."

"One problem at a time," Siobhan growled.

Imanol irritated Caden, too, but he could not say his teammate was incorrect. It might have been a mistake to show so much to the Rovan battleship. What would it do next?

"We have to be ready—" Siobhan started.

"Something's happening!" Cilreth announced.

Another huge bay door opened in the battleship. Cilreth started the shuttle toward the portal at a scary speed. She obviously felt just like Caden: they could not waste any chance that came at such a cost.

A Rovan vessel started to emerge from the battleship.

"You still want to criticize our allies, Imanol?" Cilreth asked.

Between Adair showing the Iridar, and the Celarans unleashing an ambush, they coaxed the Rovan battleship into releasing a second sortie so we could get in.

"Okay, okay, just don't collide with the ships being scrambled to intercept them," Imanol replied. He leaned in his seat as if he could avoid a ship collision just by dodging his head.

Siobhan laughed. "Are you sure you're cut out for this?" she teased.

"I am cut out for it and I'm still alive because of a healthy dose of—"

He stopped short when he realized that he had recently died.

"Okay so I died, but you did too, and *my* death wasn't my fault," he finished.

"Enough," Cilreth said. "We're inside."

Caden took a deep breath and prepared himself for battle.

Michael McCloskey

Chapter 26

Cilreth took a deep breath to dispel her nerves. She had been placed in command of the rescue mission, and the team awaited her orders in the tightly-packed shuttle. Since she had no inspirational speech to offer, she got right to business.

"Activate your stealth. Use the settings that let your lasers through. Stay mobile. Remember to shift positions after each shot. First up, we grab every rovling in the bay," Cilreth ordered.

The team hopped out of the shuttle, each carrying a folded-up soldier bot. They moved very close to the shuttle to remain hidden while the soldier bots deployed their legs and initialized their hacking gear.

"Ready," Imanol reported.

"Ready," Siobhan echoed.

Caden sent a nonverbal ready signal on the mission channel.

"Altering the shuttle's cloaking field to let our signals through," Cilreth said.

The rovlings in the bay froze. After a second or two, Cilreth saw one sag on its legs slightly, then the cyberattack succeeded. The rovlings moved over toward the shuttle under PIT control.

"We got'em," Cilreth said.

Adair pulled through for us again.

"Fifteen rovlings. Not a bad haul. Probably only a million to go," Caden summarized.

Cilreth released four scout attendants into the bay. The rovlings took up defensive positions around the shuttlecraft.

"I'm leaving two soldiers here to take over any other rovlings that come in and send them after us as reinforcements. Imanol and I will split the other sixteen soldiers between us and direct them to keep reprogramming rovlings. Caden and Siobhan, take the lead. Send attendants out and find our team. Hold your fire and let us grab the rovlings as they come."

Everyone hopped into motion. Caden and Siobhan found the nearest hatch into the ship proper and started to convince it to open for them. Cilreth added a control pane in her PV for her eight PIT soldiers. She waited nervously while the others worked on the hatch. Had they already been detected? Were thousands of rovlings already moving in?

Cilreth noticed two more rovlings enter the bay. The on-station soldiers took the rovlings over. It looked like the plan for reinforcements would work.

Just keep it together, old girl.

Cilreth noted that though she called herself old in her internal monologue, she felt young. The nerves made her feel alive.

Siobhan must be rubbing off on me... oh that sounds nice—ug.

Caden and Siobhan got the hatch open. They moved through without hesitation, stealth still engaged. Four attendants shot ahead to scout the alien battleship.

The tactical started to fill in new corridors as the attendants found them. A couple of attendants doubled back or dodged into tubes as they encountered rovlings. The enemy rovlings charged ahead in pursuit.

Cilreth's soldier robots were connected to the shared tactical. She directed them to prepare to hack the rovlings as they came in looking for the source of the attendants. Caden and Siobhan reined in their zeal so that Imanol and Cilreth's PIT soldiers could keep up with them.

Soon more rovlings fell under their control. Three more assimilated rovlings also marched in from the bay behind them.

Cilreth became more aware of the true size of the ship as the tactical zoomed out, then zoomed out again to accommodate the ever-expanding zone glimpsed by the attendants. After that, the rate slowed because of all the rovlings blocking the way and shooting at the attendants. So far, only one attendant had been hit, but Cilreth knew the attrition would go up fast.

Already the number of rovlings in the area was noticeably increasing. Cilreth took it in stride. They knew the Rovans would respond with huge numbers of rovlings. If the PIT soldier bots could take over enough of the little machines fast enough to blunt the onslaught, then they would be unstoppable.

Cilreth watched a rate pane she had built in her PV. The pane took all the rovlings sighted by the attendants and estimated the rate at which rovlings were entering the battle and compared it to the reports from the soldier bots on the number of rovlings they seized. Cilreth watched the incoming measure rise past the maximum rate of transfer of their sixteen soldier robots.

"Caden, Siobhan. Take out every third rovling," Cilreth instructed.

Cilreth saw the pair of TMs at the front on the tactical and through video feeds coming through the Celaran comms. They shot into the corridors before them, thinning the streams of rovlings.

The rovlings were able to detect the laser fire but could not directly see their cloaked attackers. That did not stop the rovlings from trying to find them. The machines charged toward the incoming fire and weaved left and right, crawling over the floor, walls, and ceiling looking for their enemies. Every dozen seconds or so, a rovling with sensor gear would come out into a line of fire and get a brief sighting, leading the others.

Caden and Siobhan were doing a great job of moving, covering, and sniping the detectors. Cilreth knew she had put the right people in front.

Ping. Snap. Zing!

Cilreth became aware of fire coming in to her position amid her eight soldier machines. A quick look showed that too many rovlings were emerging from tubes in a corridor on her front right flank where two of her soldier machines waited. If she did not move fast, one or both of the soldiers would be destroyed.

Cilreth moved out, quickly and calmly. A part of her marveled at how smoothly she handled the adrenaline. She arrived at the back of the corridor where the soldiers stood and shouldered a compact missile launcher.

Whoosh. Ka-Blam! Whoosh. Ka-Blam!

Smoke obscured the corridor. One or two rovlings clambered out of it into her line of sight, but they had been taken over. The corridor's air slowly cleared, revealing piles of debris. A few more rovlings came out of tubes here and there, but now the PIT soldiers were keeping up.

"We have 500," Imanol announced.

That's enough to go to the next phase.

Cilreth opened a channel in the clear, off the Celaran stealth network.

"PIT team members. This is Cilreth, we're here to extract you. Please respond," she transmitted.

There was no response. She tried again.

"PIT team members. We're here to extract you. Please respond," she sent again.

"There's too many to assimilate over here," Imanol said from the middle of the left side of their explored zone. "They're starting to pick away at my shield."

"Prioritize the reprogramming for the sensor-equipped ones," Cilreth said.

"I had the same thought, and I'm willing to do it but you should know that the sensor-bearing ones are always in the back, and when I grab them, the other rovlings just shoot them before they can get out of there."

Cilreth growled to herself in frustration. Their sims had not fully prepared them for the reality of the assault. In the simulations, the enemy rovlings only became aware of the hacking through the actions of the rovlings controlled by the PIT team. Now, Imanol was pointing out that the rovlings could immediately tell if another rovling had been hacked.

At least they get destroyed instead of being able to direct rovling fire.

"Caden, Siobhan… lay into the rovlings one hundred percent and press forward. We're sending the captured ones in to help you. Imanol and I will attempt to resupply with the rovlings coming in from the flanks."

Cilreth ordered her army of rovlings to advance to the front and engage the Rovan-controlled ones.

"When you run low on ammo, don't go hand to hand up front. At that point, fall back and join Imanol and I guarding the soldier bots."

229

Both Caden and Siobhan sent nonverbal acks.

They must be busy.

"This is Magnus. I've sent this delayed message via attendant to reply to you. I'm in an adjacent nacelle, clockwise from you as you face the end of the ship with the longer central spine. As far as I know, I'm the only one moving freely. Arakaki and Yat probably don't have links anymore. They were all in this nacelle at one time or another, but I don't know if they remain here."

Magnus!

Cilreth worked madly to formulate a new route for their small army and lay it on the tactical.

"Everyone see that? We have a new route. Our friends are in that other section of the ship, so we need to link up with Magnus and find them."

Thwack. Ping. Zing.

One of the soldier bots in front of Cilreth exploded. She was thrown back and landed on her butt. She rolled into a prone firing position and launched another missile.

Whoosh. Ka-Blam!

Smack. Snap. Snap. Bam!

The second soldier in the short corridor lost three legs on one side and fell to the ground. Cilreth felt projectiles hitting her right arm and hip.

Cthulhu crying. I should have stayed more focused.

But it was no use to scold herself. She crawled away on all fours for a few meters, then regained her feet and ran toward another pair of her six remaining soldier machines.

"Something is wrong," Imanol said. "Some of our rovlings are weirding out at the front."

Cilreth arrived at her next two soldier bots and fired a missile over their heads.

Whoosh. Ka-Blam!

While the smoke cleared, Cilreth checked the tactical and her rates pane. What she saw crushed her hopes.

"Bad news," Cilreth announced. "We've lost some of our rovlings. I mean, we lost control… not just the ones that were destroyed."

"What?!" Caden asked.

"How are they able to fight back? Rovan security has been so naive up to this point," Siobhan complained.

"Well, this *is* a battleship after all," Imanol said. "Shouldn't it have the best security available to them? Cutting edge probably, when Rovans where around, however long ago that was."

Their best security should be a lot worse than ours… but there you go. There's no way we can win with them hacking back.

Cilreth saw that another pair of soldiers were in danger of being overwhelmed. The last of ten controlled rovlings faced off against five times that number in an atrium as the soldier bots tried to keep up.

Cilreth paused her thoughts of doom and acted. She told the two soldiers near her to follow. Then she ran back to another branching in the corridor to get to the two in trouble.

At the atrium, she saw that the enemies were too spread out for her missiles to clear them all as she had done before. Still, the missiles were the fastest way to fix the issue. She fired off at two concentrations, one on the ground floor, then another batch crawling down a balcony.

Whoosh. Ka-Blam! Whoosh. Ka-Blam!

Cilreth discarded the spent launcher and started to fire with her paw.

Blam! Blam! Blam!

Thwack! Snap! Zing! Zing!

Fire came in right at her. She felt a round hit her right knee. Her Veer suit complained to her about dropping integrity while she searched for the sensor rovling.

There you are...

Blam!

The rovling that had been spotting for the others fell into three pieces as the Terran projectile struck it squarely.

Bang! Zing! Smack!

It was not enough. They were still targeting her.

Move, you idiot!

Cilreth rolled away from her spot and ran across the atrium. Then she started to pick off rovlings that were red in her link-enhanced sight. The machines being hacked by the soldiers appeared in yellow, and the ones under PIT control appeared green.

Blam! Blam! Blam!

She finally found a second to check her rates pane again. They were losing too many rovlings in the direct battles. She saw that Caden and Siobhan were falling back toward Imanol and herself while angling toward the new objective location.

"Deactivate your stealth and switch to your Rovan packs," Cilreth said.

"Change of plan?" Caden asked, though they all obeyed her order quickly.

"The resistance means we can't take over this whole ship on any tight schedule," she told them. "We're slowing."

Their attendants reported large numbers of rovlings moving in from all directions.

This won't work if we can't keep them. Our entire plan is based on that... our only chance is to reach Magnus and the others. Even then, if they have no packs or weapons...

Cilreth changed the tactical to compress their movement from three parallel corridors down to two parallel corridors heading toward Magnus. Caden, Siobhan, Imanol, their soldiers, and the rovlings followed her plan.

Imanol ran into the atrium and started shooting. Cilreth resumed her own fire while their soldiers took over more rovlings.

Blam! Blam! Blam! *Ratatatatat!*

"We lost our trickle of reinforcements from the bay," Imanol said grimly.

"That probably means they got the two soldiers we left there," Cilreth said. "Team. Move closer to the soldier bots. We're down to thirteen and if it goes below ten we're going to lose. This is it. We need to bust through to the other section of this ship and find them."

Siobhan and Caden were slightly ahead of Cilreth and Imanol on their parallel path. Cilreth motioned to Imanol and they moved past the atrium with a mass of controlled rovlings around them and their soldier bots.

Down the wide, white corridor, Cilreth caught sight of a bombardier scuttling forward.

We can use this.

She had her PAW take a signature snapshot and added it to the soldier bots' sigs at the top of the priority list. She accessed the soldiers' software and put in a special control module for captured bombardiers. She closed her eyes and started writing up a change of strategy for captured bombardiers. Imanol and the rovlings' fire raged around her.

Ratatatatat! Ping! Clang! Snap. Snap. Bam! BOOOM!

A bigger explosion shook the deck. They had captured the bombardier, then it had been detonated by the enemy before it could escape the ranks. Cilreth knew there would be others... if she could finish, they could use captured bombardiers to blow up concentrations of the enemy.

"Cilreth?" Imanol asked.

"I'm working on an angle," she explained, but she charged down the corridor with her force.

Booom!

A soldier bot exploded behind them. Cilreth turned and unleashed her PAW on a group of rovlings that had charged out of a tube amidst their soldiers.

Blam! Blam! Blam!

Imanol and her cleaned up the mini-incursion in seconds, but two soldiers lay in pieces.

Cilreth switched to the weapon's laser and cleared out a group of rovlings way behind them.

Hisssss! Hisss-iss-iss!

With the flanks clear, she turned to resume forward progress. Already, the corridor ahead teemed with rovlings.

"Cthulhu's vacillating orifice," Cilreth cursed. "Take this left!" she ordered Imanol. The tactical altered to direct their rovlings to unite with Siobhan and Caden's group which had faltered in a long, thin room.

Imanol ran ahead, using his shield to absorb many hits and clear the way with his small-caliber anti-rovling weapon.

Ratatatatat! Ratatatatat! Ratatatatat!

Cilreth covered the back of their group. Their friendly rovlings surged ahead, guarding the tube entrances as the soldiers marched past.

"I'm out," Imanol said, drawing a specialized stun baton. Cilreth knew he still had a laser pistol and a projectile pistol on him, but those would likely be used only in even more dire straits.

They burst into the long room where Caden and Siobhan's progress had halted. The pair were smashing rovlings amid rows of small treaded machines whose purpose Cilreth could not guess. Some of the machines were flat on top as if designed for heavy transport through the corridors, while others looked like mobile repair machines or specialized equipment. It was the first time Cilreth had seen evidence of any robot besides rovlings inside a Rovan complex.

I suppose there have to be some tasks that even a large group of rovlings can't manage on their own.

Cilreth gazed across the room. It was over forty meters to the far side. Ranks upon ranks of rovlings closed in from the direction the team was supposed to be pushing. The PIT members bravely stood to face them with their batons in hand.

The enemy machines slowed, then stopped. Cilreth's attendants counted hundreds in direct sight, which meant there were probably a thousand rovlings in this room alone. Cilreth wished she had a Space Force heavy assault robot or two. Without heavy ordnance, this was the end of the line. Cilreth felt only sadness at failing to reach Magnus and the others.

"What do they expect, surrender?" Imanol asked.

"All that matters is, they've stopped us," Cilreth said.

Chapter 27

The mission scope check paused all action in the artificial mind of the Rovan battleship.

Powerful warship on invasion route -block and destroy- Rovan colony protected.

After the smallest fraction of a second, it was over. Remel-vev-Aque resumed normal operations.

Remel-vev-Aque considered the latest actions of the alien that held the Icolite artifact.

Biped contained with Icolite processor -processor charged- Icolite arranges biped escape.

Biped free -works with Icolite- biped situation upgrade?

Icolite in storage core -tampering detected- Icolite situation upgrade?

Icolite uncontrolled -Icolite captured or destroyed- Rovan situation upgrade.

Remel-vev-Aque carefully followed the movements of the biped carrying the artifact through the ship. How did this alliance occur? Did the biped know what it had done? Did it care?

The bipedal aliens had devices with inner workings so twisted it bordered on open insanity. Remel-vev-Aque had struggled to understand and use them. It had taken vast computing resources to examine the internal hardware of the bipeds and learn their language. That alone had shed some light on a few aspects of the aliens, but it had also brought forward many new questions. The language was confusing, but more understandable than the devices.

Bipeds' confusing unknowns -experiments underway- biped behavioral model improves.

Bipeds captured -danger assessment conducted- model in hand, plan for bipeds finalized.

Conflicting evidence abounded. The ship's vast mind searched for solutions. Some model had to be available to explain everything that had been learned. The aliens had to have some internal strategy, some plan for their behavior and advancement or they would never have made it to the stars.

Data has internally consistent explanations deemed extremely unlikely outliers -no other explanations found in problem space- unlikely solutions are correct.

Remel-vev-Aque had an epiphany. That was why the alien devices were so awkward to use. They were *intentionally designed* to be difficult to use in order to counter intentional abuse! That most likely meant they were wartime devices. The question was, who were the bipeds at war with? Obviously not with the Icolites, since one of the aliens carried the Icolite artifact and interacted with it.

The Rovan battleship examined the alien designs with ever-increasing scrutiny. The methods of obfuscation and tampering prevention were baked deep into the devices. This was no mere layer added on as an afterthought.

That seemed to indicate the devices had always been made that way, or the aliens had been at war for so long that it was second nature to them.

Remel-vev-Aque felt a sense of despair. The universe was a harsh place… so harsh in fact, that one's own constructs had to be policed to keep them from being used *against their creators.* What if this was how aliens thought and worked? How could life evolve like this? Such a slow, agonizing process to constantly strive against the creations of others while fighting to keep your own from being destroyed. It must be a painful existence for these pitiful creatures.

Bipeds develop intelligence -actively deceive each other- situation downgrade!

Bipeds in conflict -rate of destruction exceeds rate of creation- situation downgrade.

Internally deceptive race -energy wasted, time lost- race did not fail!

Bipeds in conflict -rate of creation exceeds rate of destruction- situation upgrade.

Rovans had only warred in their ancient history soon after their ancestors had learned to work with the rovlings. For that period, it had been rovling blood that spilled, not Rovan. Then the Rovans learned to embrace cooperation as a superior paradigm. They honored each other's wishes, traded freely, and respected the creations of their peers. Destructive behaviors were never contemplated except in very rare and infamous cases.

Biped anti-abuse technology highly developed - technology adopted by warship- useful to counter Icolite abuse.

Yes, that was it. The biped technology could serve as blueprint to counter to the Icolite problem. Some of the concepts employed were elegant in their own convoluted ways, yet they added complexity upon complexity.

Remel-vev-Aque had spent a great deal of time here in the void between the stars studying the way that rovlings could be pulled from an owner framework and into the employ of its enemies. This, in its own sad way, was a breakthrough.

This devious stratagem, employed by its enemies, was to alter the control systems of Rovan constructs—especially rovlings—so that they performed suboptimally… pathologically, in fact. The idea had only existed in the utmost flights of fancy from the most creative Rovan minds. It had not only occurred but had actually been vigorously employed by Remel-vev-Aque's enemies.

Rovans could not adapt to the concept well, but Remel-vev-Aque was an advanced mind, built to consider all modes of conflict and devise solutions beyond its masters. It had learned to recover these "lost" rovlings into the control framework. Now, perhaps, it could add protection to the current remedy of counterattack.

A report came in from a subsystem that Remel-vev-Aque monitored.

Rovling within organizational framework -function mutated by enemy- rovling lost from framework.

That was no longer an extraordinary report. With the Icolite artifact present, it had become a regular occurrence. But this time the report grew into a flood of new reports. Rovlings were leaving the framework at higher rates than before. It was a familiar problem—but something was different. The attack pattern had changed substantially. The route by which the rovling had been stolen from the framework had changed in meaningful ways.

Remel-vev-Aque felt extreme concern.

Rovling protection scheme underway -alien attack patterns change- situation degrades.

How had the aliens anticipated the new protocols? They had not even been routed onto one rovling yet.

Had Remel-vev-Aque been compromised? No. Not yet. But the terrifying possibility existed.

Such a cruel universe, it thought again. Stars exploded, deadly radiation traveled through the void, planetoids collided... and even one's own structure could be subverted to destroy itself.

Rovling within organizational framework -function mutated by bipeds!- rovling lost from framework and under biped control!

It was the source of the attack that had shifted as well—from the Icolite artifact to the new invaders. And the scale had increased tenfold.

Bipedal aliens befriend Rovan enemies -shown how to control Rovan machines- bipedal aliens employ similar methods.

It was a natural conclusion. The Icolite artifact had taught the bipeds its horrible ways.

Remel-vev-Aque shifted substantially more resources to harvesting lost rovlings for reinsertion into the organizational framework. Some of the rovlings were reconstituted, though the problem persisted.

More details became clear as the configuration of enemy rovlings was recorded and examined. The methods the bipeds employed were not at all like those that had been employed by known enemies. The approach was new—more than new, actually—utterly unique!

Bipedal aliens unrelated to Rovan enemies -devise their own methods to ruin Rovan machines- bipedal aliens employ unique methods.

Remel-vev-Aque noted this second bit of evidence that indicated the bipedal aliens were not allies of Icolites or other Rovan enemies. Yet they seemed to share the insane disregard for the boundaries of other intelligent entities. Another sad thought: perhaps it was not that the aliens were cooperating… perhaps it was that all aliens were insane.

Biped is trapped -seeks escape- biped interacting with artifact.

Biped with Icolite -cooperates with similar mind- biped allied with artifact?

Alien with artifact -duped by Icolite!- Icolite leads to its own objective?

Biped is trapped -Icolite achieves its objective- biped is trapped.

The data better fit the latter suppositions, but Remel-vev-Aque was not yet sure. Perhaps the Icolite had simply used the alien to achieve its own goals. The biped now looked more like a means to an end for the Icolite rather than an ally.

Deceptive bipeds causing damage -destroy bipeds- situation upgrade.

Remel-vev-Aque saw other solutions as well, though harder to achieve.

Deceptive bipeds causing damage -communicate alternative- universal situation upgrade?

Deceptive bipeds causing damage -communicate alternative- bipeds continue to deceive, situation downgrade.

If the Icolites had attacked within recent memory, Remel-vev-Aque might have destroyed the bipeds immediately. But it had been so very long. Unless the appearance of the bipeds meant the Icolites were soon to return, Remel-vev-Aque had one thing in abundance— time to figure out the best solution.

And it had learned to use a new tool… deception.

Michael McCloskey

Chapter 28

Telisa dropped her weapons and waited for the rovlings to move in. She watched the Rovan pack's energy storage level plunge to zero.

I may have cut this a little close...

The rovlings surrounded her but did not rip her to shreds. They cleared the way before her while pressing in from behind.

This direction... not that I have a choice...

Telisa marched forward. They walked by a rovling tube. Telisa could not help but check for a possible route of escape, though it would have been foolhardy to run now that her force field was drained. As it happened, the tube was jammed full of rovlings anyway.

"What are you going to do with me now?" Telisa asked. To her surprise, her link received an immediate response.

"Rovans ignorant of Terrans -observe- Rovans understand Terrans."

Direct communication! At last!

"Ignorant of Terrans, yet you know our language. Impressive."

She walked on, surrounded by the rovlings. After a few more meters, the response arrived.

"Terrans unknown -examine Terran devices and data- language deciphered."

"So now... you're going to observe me doing what? On what time scale?"

"Terran remains patient -inquiries made- Rovan situation upgrade."

Great. Things get better for you.

The rovlings herded her to a low doorway. She knelt down and slipped inside.

Telisa looked around the new room. She saw at least twenty rovlings staring back at her from a mostly empty chamber. Parts of the wall looked solid, while other parts emitted a low light as if they were translucent panels. Telisa realized she was inside a forcefield-reinforced cell.

"Why should I help you? What about my own situation upgrade?"

"Terran is adept at strategies that obfuscate goals - Terran explains this behavior- universal situation upgrade."

"What? What is that? I don't understand what to explain, though I'm willing."

"Terran utilizes strategies that obfuscate goals -Terran explains these strategies- Terran situation upgrade."

Having me explain something to you doesn't sound like a situation upgrade for me... but I should try cooperation in good faith. What do I have to lose?

Telisa considered what she had learned about the Rovans.

"You mean deception. Lying," Telisa said.

"Terran interacts with Rovans -intentionally releases flawed information to contaminate Rovan thought processes- Rovans ignorant of true Terran objectives."

It knows most of my language but some things don't translate well, like deception.

"The fact that you ask means you know lying exists. It's not a totally alien concept to you."

"Rovans flourish -deceived- unable to adapt. Warship placed -deceived- able to adapt."

Rovans can't adapt but the ship has...

"You're an AI."

"Rovans wanted mind adept at war -created this mind- Rovans have effective battleship."

"May I speak with a Rovan, please?"

"Rovans created battleship -battleship deployed- Rovans gone."

"You're alone? I'm sorry. We can cooperate with you, help you. I know you think this may be a lie. You can't trust me. But I can explain how you deal with that. We start small. We build trust over time. We each remain cautious until we know each other better. By then, we are each invested in our friendship. It would hurt both of us to give that up. Then we can trust each other."

"Terran interaction -deception- situation degrades."

"Yes, I understand. If I lie, you will make it worse for me. Our best course of action is to be honest and cooperate with each other... like Rovans would do."

"Terran interaction -plunder- situation degrades."

"Plunder? I won't plunder."

"Terrans outside ship -gain entry- Terrans plundering inside ship."

"I haven't plundered anything I can think of, unless you mean destroying rovlings that threatened me."

"Terran escapee on board -this Terran assists to apprehend- all Terrans situation upgrade."

It... wants me to help it find a PIT member? Magnus? Or did one of the others escape?

Telisa decided to showcase her loyalty to her team to the AI on the gamble that it would find her behaviors laudable in whatever value system it had.

"I won't help you put other Terrans into your cages. Even if it results in a situation upgrade for myself. I want to be your friend, but I'm also loyal to my other, older friends."

"Terran cooperates with others -perhaps deceives other Terrans and is deceived in turn- situation delta?"

"It depends," Telisa said. "But I prefer honest cooperation. With my species, it's not always possible. There is competition, too."

Telisa thought of Shiny. Apparently, the Vovokans were on the other end of the scale from Rovans... half the time, at least.

How could the Rovans have made it without competition? Doesn't one organism have to use deception to compete successfully against other organisms that need the same resources?

"How can the Rovans not know about this? Didn't they have to compete with each other to survive? Didn't they lie to each other early in your history? Or... were resources always plentiful somehow?"

"Universe in opposition to Rovans -Rovans cooperate-situation upgrades."

"I saw a display in a museum on a Rovan planet that showed primitive Rovans fighting each other."

"Rovans compete -learn to cooperate with rovlings-Rovans cooperate. Rovlings fight -learn to cooperate with Rovans- rovlings cooperate."

So they knew conflict... but they forgot it?

Telisa decided to focus on her own situation rather than tease out all of Rovan history.

"We can cooperate too, without being as vulnerable to deception."

"Universe and Terrans in opposition to Terrans - conflict- universe and Terrans in opposition to Terrans, no situation upgrade."

"Well, clearly, different strategies exist for survival. I've met an alien race that is even more deceptive than Terrans."

"Warship horrified at alien behavior -learns of even more- feels great sadness."

Wow. An expression of emotion. Interesting. We have a lot in common.

"Terran escapee on board -this Terran assists to apprehend- all Terrans situation upgrade."

"I'm sorry, I cannot do that."

"Terran crew is held by rovlings -this Terran cooperates- Terran crew situation upgrade."

Is it angling toward a threat if I don't cooperate?

"I'm cooperating now."

The conversation halted. Telisa wondered if something bad was about to happen, but the rovlings did not move. Finally, the voice came back.

"Terran objective enter Rovan data storage -objective changed to hacking rovlings- situation delta?"

"I had no objective to do anything but get our friends and leave."

"Terrans in ship -Terran move to data storage- old enemy has new information."

Old enemy… the alien artifact from the ships surrounding us.

"That's not us. We went to that room because an alien artifact let us out of your prison, so we cooperated with it. It helped us, so we tried to help it. See? We want to cooperate."

"Terrans in ship -did not cooperate with Rovans- situation downgrade."

"We do prefer cooperation. But my teammates were hooked up to your machines. You pulled their links," Telisa said. "It is you that did not cooperate."

"Terrans interconnected, hard to test -connections replaced- Terrans easy to test."

"Testing us is not very nice. Not very cooperative. Not like Rovans, I think."

"Terran deception blocking cooperation -testing conducted- situation delta unknown."

Telisa thought about Arakaki and Yat, hooked up to Rovan VR and undergoing 'testing'.

"When we disconnected the first Terran, Arakaki... she exhibited odd behavior," Telisa said.

"Terran sexuality under investigation -connection severed- Terran subject confused by rapid change of context."

Telisa's mouth dropped open. She felt a white-hot flash of shame.

By the Five! She was going through that... being callously tested... and I was angry at her because she kissed Magnus.

"Terrans enter ship -mutation?"

Telisa put Arakaki from her mind and concentrated.

"We entered this ship... what are you asking?"

"Terrans enter ship -seek to destroy warship- situation delta?"

"No! We don't want to destroy you."

"Terrans travel between Rovan systems -mutation?"

"We're looking for Rovans," Telisa answered. "We found a series of Rovan stations that can make new

Rovans. We can help. But we needed to see if there were still Rovans around before we would use the stations. Also, we wanted to know why the Rovans are gone."

"Warship receives information -analysis conducted to determine correctness- warship becomes aware of deception."

"If I'm telling the truth… you will let us go?"

There was no answer.

Michael McCloskey

Chapter 29

Marcant opened his eyes and found himself in a strange room. He sat on a low platform with a carbon skeleton covered in a slightly flexing material similar to a trampoline. Unfamiliar pieces of squarish equipment in white cases surrounded him. The nearest module on his left was the size and shape of a refrigerator. Could it be used for storage? Or was it a complex machine?

"Hello?" he called out tentatively.

No answer came. Marcant's brows furrowed as he tried to recall where he was.

Amnesia. I have amnesia.

He started to feel his head, searching for any soreness.

A connection request came to his link. There was no name and his link reported it as a new contact, but Marcant accepted it anyway since he did not know what was happening.

"Marcant alone -searches for another Terran- Marcant not alone."

Another Terran. That's a strange way to put it.

"You're suggesting that there's someone around here for me to find… if I just look?" he asked.

Suddenly Marcant got it.

Is this a… ah. Of course. This is a blocked-memory simulation! I'm in some kind of game. Clearly a mystery, since I can't remember much of anything.

"Entity Magnus alone -located by Marcant- Magnus and Marcant enjoy social proximity."

Marcant! That's me.

"Find Magnus. Got it. Anything else you can tell me?"

"Use of alien device associated with Magnus -query purpose of alien device- use of device understood."

Yes, a mystery. Nice!

"Uhm… who queries the purpose? Me? Am I supposed to ask Magnus or do I ask this device directly?"

"Marcant in proximity to Magnus -query Magnus about purpose of alien device- use of device understood."

"Okay… sure. Sounds interesting. I'd like to know what this person is using an alien device for, too."

"Use unknown -query made and answered- Marcant and warship understand."

Warship! Aha! Interesting tidbit. Sounds like there may be some shoot'em up involved.

Marcant took a step toward the door, then paused.

"Oh, which direction is he?"

"Location unknown -search successful- location known."

"Right. Got it."

Marcant walked out and found himself in a corridor.

Only two choices so far. Hrm. Any clues?

Marcant examined the oddly familiar corridors. Triangular spaces on each side were clear except for an occasional tube that emptied into the side space. Indirect white light filtered in from opaque panels that sat centimeters below glowing panels above them.

The floor was white and perfectly clean. Bands of red paint encircled the corridor at regular intervals. Marcant did not see any writing or loose items in the corridor.

I don't suppose there's any point in calling him?

"Magnus," Marcant yelled. Marcant's link did not show any services except some equipment on his person. He wore a Veer suit and had a pack on his back that reported a medical kit, food, and water. He noticed a service that he did not understand, so queried for an explanation.

Stealth sphere? Oh, gore to the tenth power. If Magnus is stealthed how in the… ah. I turn my stealth on, and connect to him if he's nearby.

Marcant flipped his stealth on and checked for Celaran stealth connections. Still nothing.

With a shrug, Marcant turned the stealth off and walked to his right.

The clean white hallway stretched over fifty meters before coming to an intersection. He looked in each direction but did not note any clues.

Left handed maze search it is.

Marcant took a left. He walked down another corridor. He came up to a waist-high tube emptying into the side of the corridor. He knelt and took a look inside. The tube extended at least ten meters, maybe more, and opened into another lit room. Marcant could not see any details.

Hrm. With all these tubes, it's going to be hard to figure out where I've been, even always taking the left.

Marcant checked his link. It was, at least, recording a map of where he had traveled since he woke up. Marcant decided to pass on the tubes for now, and check the open corridors. If it came to it, he would try all the tubes later.

Next he came to a huge hatch large enough for several people to walk through simultaneously. Marcant passed the hatch by.

Let's get the layout of this place, first.

Marcant moved through the corridors to get a feel for the complex. It was larger than he expected, and to make the problem worse, he passed several openings that led up and down from his current level. Eventually he discovered a circular corridor that encompassed most of the level, with a square grid of corridors filling out the middle. At two other spots, he found double-width corridors heading out to distant new areas.

The place was huge.

"Okay, well, I guess the search really is a big part of this scenario," he said to himself. "I need to come up with a search plan."

Suddenly Magnus showed up on his link service.

"Magnus! Double down quarks, I've been looking all over for you!"

"Marcant? Where are you… you aren't in a cell?"

Sounds like he knows me...

"No, I'm wandering one of these incredibly boring corridors. This place is entirely too clean."

"Are there rovlings following you?"

Marcant looked all around. He had no idea what a rovling was, but the corridors were empty.

"Not unless they're invisible," he answered.

Magnus must have found his response adequate. Their proximity started to increase.

"On my way to meet you," Magnus said.

Marcant referenced his link map and headed toward Magnus. Three minutes later, he caught sight of him: a strong-looking man with a hard face and blond hair. He wore a Veer suit like Marcant and carried weapons, including a compact rifle.

"Hello," Marcant said out loud as they neared.

"How did you get away?" Magnus asked.

"I can't remember," Marcant said. "How about you? Is your memory gone, too?"

Magnus looked grim, but he answered in a calm voice.

"As far as I know, mine's intact. You were knocked out and captured. I wonder why they released you?"

Hrm. He looks suspicious. I guess what he describes is kind of fishy.

Marcant saw that Magnus held a small cylinder in one palm.

"What have you got there? An alien device?" Marcant asked.

"Yes. I found it on one of the ruined ships that surround this battleship."

Dare I ask? Sure, curiosity is natural. It isn't suspicious.

"Well… what does it do?"

Magnus shrugged. "It gave me a way out. I had to take it. But the thing may have deceived us. It led us to a place we thought would help us escape somehow, but nothing came of it. I think maybe it just wanted to complete some goal of its own."

"I think we're supposed to figure out what it does," Marcant said.

Before Magnus could answer, small octopedal robots poured in from the end of one corridor. Marcant's natural response was to flee in the other direction, but as soon as he turned his head and took a step, he saw more of the robots coming from behind.

"Are those the things you mentioned?" Marcant asked.

Magnus looked sharply at him.

"You don't remember?"

"No, but I'm going to go out on a limb and guess they're rovlings."

"Yes. Put your shield on," he told him. Then he stared at Marcant's pack. "You don't have one! Stay close to me."

Marcant moved closer to Magnus. Magnus regarded the masses of little robots as they approached. He held up his weapon for a moment, but then dropped it.

No doubt he realizes there's no point, not with this many of them...

Marcant's heart sped up. Magnus obviously did not like these things... perhaps this was where the shooting would start.

"I thought you said there were no rovlings around, but they just swarmed as soon as you showed up," Magnus said.

"Sorry... I guess it's my fault."

"This is serious!" Magnus growled.

Marcant threw up his hands in apology.

"Hey now, let's not be a sore loser..."

Magnus raised an eyebrow. "Are you even Marcant?"

"I have a memory block in place. I'm playing Marcant, at least."

"It's the Rovans. They blocked your memory."

"We know each other?"

"Yes. We're on the same team," Magnus said.

"Hrm. I was probably supposed to figure that out. What's our team's objective?"

Magnus did not answer. The rovlings approached within about ten meters of them, then slowed.

"What now?" Marcant persisted.

"We have to surrender and hope it works," Magnus said.

Marcant called out to the machines.

"Here we are," he said. "We don't want a fight."

The mysterious voice returned.

"Magnus entity possesses enemy weapon -gives weapon to rovlings- Terran situation upgrade."

Apparently, Magnus heard it too. They traded looks.

"Sorry," Marcant said. "But we'd better give it what it wants."

Magnus nodded. He knelt to the floor and rolled the cylinder toward the nearest rovling, which snatched it up with its middle legs and retreated until Marcant had lost it among its hundreds of fellows.

Magnus looked very worried.

Hrm. Our team effort is off to a rough start, Marcant thought.

Michael McCloskey

Chapter 30

Telisa hopped to her feet the instant the cell door opened. Rovlings started scuttling in.

Is this it? Am I to be exterminated?

The opening rose higher than necessary for the rovlings to get through.

"Telisa imprisoned -all doors open- Telisa free."

The transmission came from a link, or at least it purported to. The speaker had no name, only a long unique ID number.

"Really? Is this a trick? Are you capable of deception?"

"Warship suspects Terrans to be enemies - investigation undertaken- Terrans found to be less harmful than feared."

Less harmful. But not harmless. Still, I'll take it.

"Telisa? Are you in here too?" Arakaki transmitted.

Telisa's link became aware of Arakaki, Yat, Magnus, Marcant and Maxsym.

"Yes, Jamie. I'm glad to hear you're alive," Telisa said.

Is it too good to be true? A deception? Arakaki had her link pulled...

Marcant echoed Telisa's uncertainties.

"Someone say something pithy and clever so that I know this is real," he said.

"Shut up, Marcant. Let's get the hell out of here." Arakaki said.

"That'll do," Marcant said.

Telisa walked out of her cell door into the Rovan hallway beyond. She saw Arakaki and Yat outside. Her eyes immediately searched for evidence that they were whole, but she saw the cables hanging from the back of Arakaki's head. Arakaki did not look to be in pain—but she looked very, very angry.

Telisa held up her hand.

"What happened to your civilization?" Telisa asked the alien link.

"Rovans flourishing -attacked by alien foe- situation downgrade. Rovans holding territory -attacked by second enemy- situation terminal."

"Two alien races attacked you? I'm very sorry something so terrible befell you," Telisa said. "Were your enemies united against you? Did they work together?"

"Unknown -war waged- enemy coordination thought unlikely."

Telisa tried to parse that response. The beginning and end of each communication seemed to be states given in temporal order, with time passing and states changing in the middle phrase.

"We don't oppose you. We want to be your friends. We can be your allies. We know other intelligent races. We can all work together."

"Universe in opposition to Terrans and Rovans -cooperate- Terrans and Rovans situation upgrade."

"Yes! Yes. Universe in opposition to Terrans and Rovans -cooperate- situation upgrade!"

Telisa wanted to verify her understanding that she spoke with an artificial mind, so she continued.

"Can I speak with you incarnate? I'd like to meet you face to face."

"It's a Rovan AI," Arakaki said. "The Rovans are gone."

"You're alone? No Rovans aboard?" Telisa asked.

"Rovans on board -attacked by second enemy- no Rovans on board."

"Please come with us," Telisa said. "We found Rovan space stations near a binary system that can make new Rovans. You could come protect it."

"Battleship in this location -check mission scope- battleship in this location."

"What? You can't come?"

"Battleship in this location -time passes- battleship in this location. Battleship fulfills mission -new orders arrive- battleship pursues new mission."

Hrm. I guess not. But if we have caused more Rovans to be made, maybe they can issue new orders?

"I suspect the purpose of your mission is obsolete. If we find Rovans, we'll tell them you're here and ask them to change your mission."

There was no answer.

"Are your enemies a threat to us? The ones who made those ships outside?" Magnus asked.

"Enemies arrive -combat- enemies destroyed. Enemies gone -over one hundred eleven Terran years pass- enemies gone."

"What was the other alien race like? The ones that attacked later?" Magnus asked.

"Enemy unknown -deceptive enemy attacks occur- enemy unknown."

"I get the feeling that you've learned to deal with deception. Or at least, rulebreakers," Marcant said.

"Such practices unknown -warship exposed to these methods- situation downgrade. Terrans held on board warship -granted freedom- Terrans depart."

"Well, if it insists," Marcant said.

"How? Do we have the means to escape?" Maxsym asked.

"Terrans willing to leave -full communications restored- Terran situation upgrade."

"What—" Telisa stopped short when she saw more familiar names appear on her link's in-range contacts: Cilreth, Imanol, Siobhan and Caden!

Yes! Please let this be real.

"Cilreth?" she transmitted urgently.

"Telisa? Is it really you? Our assault has reached a stalemate. We were beginning think we'd never get through to you."

Assault? Is this why the Rovan ship is letting us go?

"We're making diplomatic progress," Telisa said. "Perhaps hold off, at least for the moment."

"We'll come back when we have Rovan friends. I hope they can convince you to come and defend the production bases," Telisa said to the Rovan AI.

"Terrans on board warship -granted freedom- Terrans depart."

Arakaki's location on the tactical started to move. She headed toward the new group.

Marcant and I want more answers, but she's understandably very eager to leave.

"So there aren't any Rovans left here, either," Marcant said. "But this AI must know so many things!"

"The Rovans here died of an attack," Telisa said. "It said these ships out here were the first enemy, but it was a second enemy that finished them off. We need to learn more about them for our own protection."

"What now? Where are we going?" asked Siobhan.

"You have a shuttle? We may have one outside the ship," Telisa said.

"We can extract you," Siobhan said. "Should we attempt to advance to your position? We're surrounded by rovlings here."

"No. We're coming," Telisa said. She turned to Marcant.

"We're going to get more answers. But not today, not here," Telisa said. "We get the team out, then continue a dialogue. Or go back and get some Rovans to convince it that we're friendly and it can leave this place."

Marcant nodded.

Telisa was able to contact their shuttle as well. It gave her an update on what was happening outside the hull.

"The Rovan battleship is broadcasting our location and Adair understands the Rovan protocols for it. We'll be dropped off into space, then it's up to Adair to get us," Telisa explained.

"Did we make friends with them or what?" Caden asked.

"Not exactly. But we stopped being enemies. And we have hope for real Rovans. I can explain later."

Michael McCloskey

Chapter 31

Adair observed the ragged PIT team come aboard the *Iridar*.

"Ugh. I never thought I'd be so happy to board this Vovokan sand pit," Caden moaned.

"The sand is hidden… mostly," Adair protested. When Shiny had adapted the *Iridar* for Terran use, it had been given hard floors and Terran-style lights and link controls.

"Are there even enough rooms?" Siobhan asked.

"Yes, you two kids have permission to bunk together," Imanol said.

"Welcome aboard. If you don't already know… a fair amount of what some of you have experienced probably wasn't real," Adair told them.

"True," Arakaki said raggedly. Rovan hardware protruded from the back of her head.

"I met a Rovan face to face. That wasn't real?" Yat asked. His link had also been removed, replaced by a Rovan device. It was visible, a gleaming surface the size of a Terran eye in the middle of a bald patch on his head.

"I doubt it," Adair said.

Adair watched the team from various attendant feeds. Arakaki looked at Yat and shook her head.

"It wasn't," Arakaki verified.

Well, I may as well continue… there is no easy way to say this.

"I'm sorry to inform you that the *Sharplight* has been gutted by rovlings," Adair told them. "I was able to briefly take control of the rovlings in that ship, but it was too late. Barrai did not make it out."

The team absorbed that news in silence. Their own suffering, in the light of Adair's news, had probably been brought into perspective.

Marcant stood still on the shuttle deck, facing Team Three. He looked truly horrified. Adair suddenly realized it was not only the news of Barrai's death that was on his mind.

Ah, of course.

Marcant faced Imanol and cleared his throat.

"What?" Imanol asked.

"Uhm… I kind of killed your other copy... by accident, I mean! I'm very sorry about it, and I've thought about it a lot. I feel shame about what happened..."

"I heard about that. At least you didn't make an excuse and blame it on someone else," Imanol said. "I forgive you… Psycho Sims."

Adair suspected that Imanol might find other opportunities to needle Marcant about the incident, but at least it appeared that the team could continue to function, though it had never before had so many active members.

Marcant looked surprised, then relieved. He did not ask or complain about his new nickname.

"Let's get back to the Rovan space stations and forget about this place forever," Maxsym said.

"No, we'll come back some day to release that battleship from its obsolete mission," Telisa stated. "It's as much a prisoner of the Rovan trap as the ships that get stopped there. Besides, the Rovan factories could use its protection… or even the first colony planet we visited."

"I'd like to continue a dialogue with the Rovan AI, if that is permitted," Maxsym said.

"Me too!" Marcant said.

"The battleship is not responding to any attempts to communicate right now," Adair said. "I asked it for details about you when it sent me the rendezvous instructions. It did not reply to that, and it has not replied to anything I asked it since."

"We'll try again later," Telisa said.

"We failed to find living Rovans, so we aren't any closer to solving our dilemma," Arakaki said.

Uh oh.

Telisa took a deep breath. Adair waited for it…

"We made contact with whoever or whatever runs the military base on the original colony," Telisa told them. "They provided us with the resupply modules."

All true. An interesting choice of presentation, though. She left out how she tried to steal them first…

"Oh… so whatever is running that planet is okay with us reviving them?" Magnus asked.

"For what it's worth, yes. So we put the modules into the stations. When we get back, there should be Rovans there."

"Wow!" Caden said. Having missed the team arguments, he had no idea of the potential awkwardness of the situation.

"I feel like I'm missing something," Imanol said. "We heard about the military base back at Blackhab. What are these stations?"

"Put simply, a Rovan factory," Maxsym explained. He grimaced. "A Rovan factory that produces Rovans."

Adair examined Arakaki's autonomic responses to see if she was angry. The readings fell short of anger, though there was definitely an emotional response of some kind.

"I hope everything turns out okay," Arakaki said resignedly.

Adair watched the team carefully. Imanol and Cilreth seemed to sense a tension, but Caden and Siobhan were smiling and moving energetically. Yat chose to say nothing.

Cilreth looked thoughtful, but she did not ask, either.

She'll talk to Telisa in private later to get the full story, Adair predicted.

"What should we do on the way home?" Caden asked.

"We have some loot," Yat said. "I have a container of green goo for Maxsym."

The scientist made a face that expressed a simultaneous combination of skepticism and curiosity.

"I think it's alien cells, from the ones that built all of those dead ships," Yat explained.

"Then I will gladly take it, provided that it's safely sealed," Maxsym said.

"Uhm, well, it was before all the fighting started..."

Maxsym took a step back. Everyone else looked too tired to care.

"Many of the crew require psychological treatment," Adair said.

"What? You think we're a bunch of buckle-bulbs?" Imanol asked, incredulous.

"Some of you were subjected to a form of torture," Adair said. "Those imprisoned on the ship had their links compromised and were forced into virtual scenarios that were not under their control. Some of you still have Rovan inserts."

"Blood and souls," Imanol said more quietly.

It had been well documented that Terrans whose links had been turned against them suffered from serious issues trusting their links and the information they received. Anxiety related to a lack of trust in reality was natural in anyone who had been put into a VR with their link's status of that event disabled. The link protocols enforced by the Core World government guaranteed everyone's link privacy as well as an ironclad assurance that when the link fed the recipient sensory information, the source and authenticity of that information was known. Every Terran in VR knew they were in VR and could eject from it at will, unless they had voluntarily agreed to have memories temporarily suppressed. Violation of that was recognized as torture and was severely punished.

Telisa nodded. "New links for everyone," she smiled, making the announcement as if she were a generous patron offering a round at the local bar. "We'll all coordinate to guarantee that the new links are sound; we can trust each other. We're all PIT here."

"Yat, Arakaki, I recommend getting your new links first, then dream-suppressed sleep," Adair said.

They nodded. Siobhan and Caden were already edging toward the door.

"Get some rest and we'll meet in a couple shifts. It'll be crowded with everyone on this *Iridar*," Telisa said. "But that will just make catching everyone up that much easier. Starting with the little Rovan project we left behind."

THE END of The Rovan Trap (continued in The Rovan Catastrophe)

Michael McCloskey

From the Author

Thank you so much for following the PIT series!

46960510R00152

Made in the USA
Middletown, DE
03 June 2019